LAURIE HALSE A...

Acting Out

SCHOLASTIC INC.

ISBN 978-0-545-53065-1

12 11 10 9 8 7 6 5 4 3 2 1   13 14 15 16 17/0

Printed in the U.S.A.   40

First Scholastic printing, December 2012

Text set in Joanna MT

Chapter One

· · · · · · · · · · ·

You're dumping me again, Mom."

"Zoe, don't be dramatic."

Mom sits at Gran's kitchen table and doesn't take her eyes off me. I lean against the counter, cross my arms, and roll my eyes to the ceiling.

"Zoe, it would be different if we were filming this movie only during the summer. But it's going to take months. You can't be out of middle school that long. Once summer starts, you can visit me for a week or two on set in Vancouver."

Visit. What does that mean? I guess Mom expects to be in Canada through the summer, but how long after that? And why can't I spend the whole summer with her?

Mom takes a tiny bite out of her Pop-Tart and washes it down with a gulp of coffee. She doesn't usually eat sugary stuff like that, but here at Gran's house there's no organic yogurt in the fridge, and the bananas on her counter are rounding the corner from deep brown to black. Pop-Tarts for breakfast it is. I'm not even remotely hungry, though. Mom wrinkles her nose and takes another bite.

We just arrived late last night and Mom is already leaving again. She's continuing on to New York City. We used to live there together. Then I moved to Ambler before joining Mom in California, and now it's back to Ambler again—for me, at least. In New York, Mom is meeting once more with the movie's costume designer and checking in with some of her old soap-opera friends. They're my friends, too, and I don't see why I can't at least make the trip to New York before settling in to life in Ambler, Pennsylvania, again.

I try one more time. "Why can't I just spend the weekend in New York with you before you fly to Vancouver? I can take the train back here by myself, you know I can."

"We've gone over and over this. You know I promised your grandmother that I would deliver you here. New York will be much too hectic. I wouldn't have time to have fun with you; I have too much to fit in before we start shooting—"

"But it's spring break here this week!" I say. "I wouldn't even be missing school."

"Which is why this is so perfect. You'll have a little time to settle back in with Gran and Maggie before having to start school again."

Mom gets up from the table and hugs me. A car horn blares out front.

"That's my cab. Listen, Zoe, we'll check in with each other every day or so. Once I'm on set it might be a little more time between calls or emails. But I promise we'll stay in touch, okay? Of course we will." Mom squeezes me hard and kisses my cheek. Her breath smells like strong coffee and even stronger peppermint. She gathers up her bags and sweeps toward the door.

"Tell my mother good-bye for me. I can't wait around until she's finished with whichever four-legged friend she's tending to now!" She waves as she leaves.

"I love you," I hear Mom sing out after the door has closed behind her.

I sigh. Stranded again. Left behind by Mom because she has bigger plans than me. I guess I might as well go back to bed. I'm still pretty tired from traveling, and I don't exactly feel ready to face this new—er, old—life. I'm heading back to my old bedroom when I hear my name. It's my cousin Maggie. I can hear her talking to a boy and a girl whose voices I don't recognize. I pause, standing behind the kitchen door separating Gran's house from her vet clinic.

"Late," Maggie says. "Really late. Gran picked up Zoe and Aunt Rose from the airport after midnight. Their plane was delayed. Gran let me stay up so I could say hi to them. I think Aunt Rose has already left. She had to be in New York City this morning."

"Wow. It must be a big change, going from Hollywood back to living in Ambler. Does she seem different to you?" the girl asks.

"Zoe? Not much. Even jet-lagged Zoe is pretty dramatic." The way Maggie says it I'm not sure if she means that in a good way or not. I love her, but Maggie and I haven't always gotten along.

"But who knows. Gran pretty much sent us right to bed," Maggie continues. "Then she and Aunt Rose stayed up talking. I think Zoe is still sleeping, but you'll meet her at some point today."

"Do you look alike?" the girl asks.

"They're cousins, not twin sisters!" the boy says.

"We look nothing alike," Maggie begins. "Well, she does have a little MacKenzie red in her long blond hair. But no freckles like me. And she dresses . . . she dresses . . . well, different. You'll see."

What does Maggie mean by "*different*"? I just look neat and tidy. Okay, and rather stylish. I think about the three extra suitcases I begged Mom to let me bring, brimming with new jeans, sparkly shirts, and an embarrassing number of shoes. Maggie, I am sure, must look like her usual red-headed, flannel shirt–wearing self. She could look so much better if she just took a minute with her hair or cared a tiny bit about her clothes—and not just about whether they were clean or not. But all Maggie cares about is basketball and animals. Which are both great, but maybe she'll finally let me give her some style tips this time around. Maybe.

"How long will she be staying?" the girl asks.

"I have no idea," Maggie says with a funny voice. I wish I had seen her face when she said that. "Maybe the rest of the school year and the whole summer? Her mom's filming in Vancouver will probably take about that long," she continues.

"I can't believe her mom is a movie star," the girl says.

"I don't think you could call her a movie star, but she's an actress, anyway."

What?? I would definitely call my mother a movie star! Well, okay, maybe not yet. But she is a star of this movie, anyway.

"My aunt is really pretty," Maggie adds. "Zoe is, too."

Aw, that's nice. I'm about to go show them what I look like when I hear the boy ask, "Are you happy she's back? Will it be weird to share your grandmother again?"

Yeah, I sure do want to hear the answer to this one.

I listen closely. I hear only the metallic sound of cage doors opening and closing. The kids must have moved into the recovery room to clean cages. It's Saturday morning, and I know that is on Gran's Vet Volunteers to-do list.

I open the door a tiny bit to try to hear better. I know they can't see me here, but their voices are still muffled.

"Are you coming in to help, or are you going to stand at the door all day?" The voice startles me. Standing behind me is Dr. J. J. MacKenzie, owner of Dr. Mac's Place Veterinary Clinic to everybody here in Ambler, Pennsylvania. But to Maggie and me, she's just Gran, wonder woman caretaker of orphaned granddaughters. Maggie, fulltime since her parents died in a car crash. And me, any time my mom's acting career is more important than I am.

"Zoe?" Gran examines me. "Still sleepy?" she asks.

"No, I'm fine."

"Welcome back," Gran says, holding the door wide.

"It's good to be back," I say. I walk in with a small smile, but I don't really mean it. There's a lot about Ambler to love, but right now, it just feels like a place where I keep ending up—a place that isn't my real home.

" 'Bout time you showed up to clean," Maggie says, her head deep in a large kitten crate on the floor. Through the cage wires I can see her grin.

"Hi, I'm Josh Darrow," says the boy in the corner. He's about my age and has friendly brown eyes and slightly curly brown hair. He has on the gloves Gran makes us wear when we clean around here.

"This is Jules, my sister. We're the newest Vet Volunteers." Josh sweeps his yellow-gloved arm toward a girl holding a teeny gray kitten. The brother and sister look about the same age. She has the same brown eyes and the same color hair. Maybe they're twins?

"Hi," the girl says shyly.

"Hi. I'm Zoe," I say, like that isn't obvious. Of course they know who I am. Still, everyone just smiles. Even Gran.

"Okay," Gran begins, "if we're finished with the

cleaning, let's have Maggie and Josh exercise our boarder dogs and Jules can show Zoe what we're doing with those kittens." Gran moves on to a mountain of paperwork on the counter. It's a mess. Some things never change.

"We have some little-bitties here," Jules says, bending over Maggie's now-clean kitten crate and settling the gray kitten into it. "Three of them are on bottles now, but not the two littlest ones. Have you used this before?" Jules holds up the eyedropper that we use to feed the smallest, weakest animals.

"I have," I say, heading to the sinks to scrub my hands, wrists, and forearms. It's all about safety at Dr. Mac's Place, and safety begins with cleanliness, as Gran always says.

Jules and I work in silence for a while. We feed the two tiny kittens with the eyedropper and the three healthier kittens with small bottles. Jules had filled all the bottles with formula and set them on the warmer pad before we began. After each kitten is fed, we wipe the corners of their eyes, their mouths, and noses with a small, moistened gauze pad. We check their fur all over to be sure they are clean and don't have any mites or fleas. And then we tuck each one back in under the heat lamp in the clean kitten crate.

I can feel Jules sneaking looks at me as she tends to her kitten, but she doesn't say anything. It seems like she's shy. Maybe it's up to me to make conversation.

I gently scoop up one of the two tiny kittens from the crate and ask, "So, are you and Josh twins or just close in age?" The kitten opens and closes her mouth quickly, expecting, I guess, the eyedropper of milk. Her tiny tongue searches for more, and I keep squeezing, drop by drop. I've missed all this in California. My dog, Sneakers, doesn't need any help with feeding—he loves to eat! I wish I could have brought him with me this time. I miss that little short-haired mutt. But our neighbor, Mr. Gregory, is taking care of him. He has three dogs of his own, so I guess one more is no big deal to him. I hope he's able to give Sneakers some extra love with all those other dogs around.

"We're twins," Jules says. I'm slightly startled. I'd already forgotten that I'd asked a question.

I wait for Jules to tell me more about herself. But she doesn't say anything else. She expertly moves on to her next kitten, cuddling the kitten beneath her chin before placing the bottle's nipple in its mouth. The two just-fed kittens are sleepy and are curled up together. Another kitten is stumbling around the box, and Jules and I each have one in our hands. Five kittens. Tiny and motherless. Poor things.

"Have you been in Ambler long?" I ask.

"About a month," Jules replies. Her kitten is a little squirmy. Jules stops feeding her a moment and rubs her tummy to "burp" her. Then she tries giving her the bottle again. The kitten settles and feeds. Jules sure knows her way around animals.

"And you managed to become a Vet Volunteer so fast?" Gran must be busier than when I left a year ago if she's taken on two more volunteers.

"I was a volunteer at the animal shelter back in Pittsburgh where we lived before. I'm used to working with animals." Jules cuddles her kitten and puts her back in the box.

She picks up the last kitten and does her cuddle thing again. This one is mewing as loudly as she can. Jules gently shushes her as she brings the nipple to the kitten's mouth. The kitten laps at the milk and closes her eyes.

My kitten has not eaten enough. She's the smallest, one of the ones we need to use the dropper with. I check the dropper to see how much she's had. Not nearly enough. But she has fallen asleep in my hands.

"Try blowing gently in her face. That might

wake her up without scaring her," Jules says quietly.

I raise the kitten up to my face. It's too bad I have to wake her. She looks so sweet and peaceful. But I take Jules's suggestion and blow gently. The kitten's whiskers move in the breeze. But she stays asleep. Her calico fur is like a dandelion puff, soft and barely there. In fact, she herself is barely there: she weighs almost nothing at all.

"What do you think?" I ask Jules. "Should I just let her sleep?"

"I'd give it another try. She's the smallest, and Dr. Mac is worried that she might not make it. Meow at her, too. That might wake her up enough to eat," Jules suggests.

Meow at her? That seems a little silly. I look into the box, and the three kittens are sleeping in a little pile. Jules adds the fourth one, all done eating now. The kitten curls up with the others and falls asleep, too. I look carefully at the one in my hand, and now I see that she really is the smallest by a lot. Her breathing looks shallower than the others, too.

"Is she sick?" I ask.

"Not that we know of, just tiny. The whole litter was abandoned in the grocery store parking lot. Sunita found them. Do you know her?" Jules asks.

"Of course. Sunita was a Vet Volunteer before I was. And she sure loves cats! She must have flipped when she found abandoned kittens."

"Yeah, she was pretty mad. Who dumps a box of newborn kittens at the grocery store and walks away? Dr. Mac had to calm Sunita down just to get the box out of her hands. But Sunita is right. What kind of person does that?"

What kind of person abandons *anyone*? A daughter, for instance. How come any time my mother has an acting job I get left behind? She should have taken me with her. She shouldn't have abandoned me again.

"Do you want me to try?" Jules asks.

"What? Try what?" I don't understand.

"Feeding that calico," Jules says.

"Oh yeah, sure," I say, handing her over. I forgot what I was doing. I got totally distracted, thinking about my mom again. Then I hear another familiar voice.

"I wonder if you're still a little jet-lagged." It's Gran. Where did she come from? "Do you need more sleep?" she presses, giving me a hard look.

"No, I'm fine," I reply. "Really!"

"Well, if you're sure about that, I think Maggie and Josh are heading over to David's to see his new cat. We're about done here if you two want to join them." Gran closes the cage on another cat, one who has obviously had some surgery on her belly by the looks of the stitches and the cone-shaped Elizabethan collar around her neck. Most animals hate those plastic collars, but it keeps them from tearing out their stitches.

Gran bends down and croons, "You're a good girl, Miss Taffy, such a good girl." The cat blinks at Gran and then closes her eyes. Lots of sleeping going on around here this morning. Maybe I should go back to sleep. Then I wouldn't have to think about Mom.

Jules has finally fed my kitten. She smiles at me as we clean and sterilize the droppers. Loud voices come from the front of the clinic. I recognize them all. In just a minute, I see two of my old friends round the corner.

"Zoe! It's so great to see you," Brenna Lake says. Click! She snaps my picture.

"Hey! I'm still in my pajamas! Don't you dare take any more pictures," I say, reaching back and smoothing my hair.

"Come on silly, that's why they're called candids! I'm glad you're back. Cute pj's." Brenna clicks again. Ok, I'll admit that my leopard-print matching pajamas are pretty adorable, but still. I'd better go change.

"We're all so happy that you're back. We missed you!" Sunita says, her dark eyes wide and smiling. Sunita Patel means everything she says, so I feel extra welcomed. I just wish I could be happy to be back, too. But right when I start to feel sad again, a bell jingles and the door bursts open. Maggie and Josh rush in.

"Okay, the dogs are all exercised and in their kennels. Let's get to David's!" Maggie says, flipping her ponytail behind her back. "His mom has lunch for all of us."

"Yum, let's go," Brenna says.

"Thanks for your help, Josh and Jules, Maggie and Zoe. And I'll see Brenna and Sunita sometime this week," Gran calls from her paperwork. Poor Gran. The pile does not seem any smaller.

"Hang on, guys," I say. "Let me get changed. I'll be right back."

I rush upstairs and throw on one of my new pairs of jeans with a lime green sweater and matching ballet flats. I give myself a quick glance in the mirror and add a necklace of multicolored glass beads. It's nothing too special, but I'm short on time. I run a comb through my hair, grab a lip gloss and rejoin the rest of the group.

We head across the street to David's house. I'm glad my first day back is one with all the Vet

Volunteers. Everyone seems excited to see me. But I sure do wish I knew whether Maggie was happy to have me back or not.

I take a hard look at my cousin to see if I can find the answer in her face, but she is busy twirling the cat toothbrush Gran sent along for David's cat at Sunita. Josh, Jules, and Brenna are talking about some Stream Cleanup Day they did. And I just trail behind, wondering how I'll fit back in—if I'll fit back in—with this tight group of friends: the Vet Volunteers.

Chapter Two

• • • • • • • • • • • •

"Come on, come on, come on!" David says, opening the door. "Just wait till you see this cat. Oh hey, Zoe. Um. Nice to see you." David Hutchinson hasn't changed at all. His hair is as messy as the stained sweatshirt he's wearing and he's talking fast. "Let's go upstairs. He's in my room," David continues as he rushes us into the house and past the kitchen.

"Hi, kids," Mrs. Hutchinson calls out. "I'm making mini pizzas."

We stop in the hall. Mrs. Hutchinson has drinks and paper plates lined up on the kitchen counter.

"I hope you all like them." She looks at me.

"Welcome back, Zoe. Do you eat pizza? I can fix you a salad if you prefer."

"I like pizza," I reply. I usually eat healthier food than that, but I don't want Mrs. Hutchinson to see me as some kind of problem child. The refrigerator door behind her closes and I see a cute older boy drinking milk straight from the carton. Oh, wow. It's Brian. David's older brother has turned into somebody who belongs on the cover of *Entertainment Weekly*. I check my sweater and my hair to make sure they're both smoothed down.

Mrs. Hutchinson looks at me and back at Brian. Then she raises an eyebrow and chuckles. "Lunch will be ready in about fifteen minutes, David."

"Cool, thanks, Mom!" David says and leads the way once again to his room. When we enter, his cat is curled up on his bed.

Sunita, of course, is the first to pull Rover into her arms. "Ohhh, such a pretty cat," she purrs at him, cuddling the tabby on her lap.

Click. Brenna takes a picture. "That'll be a good one," she says. Now I'm happy she brought her camera. Maybe she can get a picture of Brian before we leave, too. Wonder how I can suggest that?

Brenna stands on a chair and aims the camera

straight down at Sunita and Rover. Click. Then she lies down on the floor and gets one from that angle. Click. Rover turns his head at the sound of the camera. Then he bats a paw at it.

"That's my guy." David grins.

Maggie laughs and holds her arms out to Rover. Sunita quickly hands him over, even though she looks a little sad to give him up. But in Maggie's arms Rover isn't so calm. He twists to get free.

"Okay, little boy, you can explore," Maggie says. She sets Rover on the floor, and Brenna takes another shot. Rover's on his hind legs now with his front paws on Brenna's camera. He is so cute. Click.

"That's going to be your close-up, Rover!" Brenna says.

Maggie, Sunita, and I sit down on the floor. Josh and Jules stay standing by the door—they still seem a little shy around the group, or at least Jules does. Brenna keeps moving all over the place to get her pictures. David belly flops on his bed and clucks his tongue at Rover.

"Okay, now watch this," David says, pulling a toothbrush out of his sweatshirt pocket. "Sit." Rover sees it *and sits*. Sits! Like a dog waiting for a treat.

"Man," David says. "Rover's the craziest cat

ever. Check this out." He tosses the toothbrush over his head toward his closet door. Rover takes off running. Once he reaches the toothbrush he scoops it up in his mouth and brings it right back to David. We all applaud. David hoots like he's at a basketball game. Rover darts around David and jumps back on the bed.

"Fantastic!" Sunita says.

David nods. "We had to get him his own toothbrush so he'd stop swiping ours!"

"What a crazy cat!" Maggie beams. "Oh, before I forget, Gran sent you this toothbrush. It's specially designed for cats, and is smaller than a human toothbrush—in case Rover gets tired of carrying that big one around. And, you know, in case you want to actually brush his teeth." My cousin hands over the skinny brush.

"How'd you teach a cat to fetch?" Brenna asks.

"He knew how already," David answers. "I wish I had taught him. That would have been cool. I'm going to try to teach him other doggy tricks like rolling over and begging."

"Do it again," Brenna says. "I want to get an action shot."

David takes the toothbrush from Rover's mouth. Rover sits. And waits. David tosses it again and Rover goes running.

Josh and Jules are looking at the cat and whispering. I wonder what's up with that. I hear one of them say something like "backdoor cat."

"But I didn't know he could fetch," I hear Jules say.

David must have heard her, too. "What about a backdoor cat?" he says.

"Jules used to take care of this cat when he was at our place," Josh says.

"Your place?" David asks.

"Where did you get the cat?" Josh asks.

"What, do you think I took your cat?" David stands and looks worried. "I didn't know you even had a cat, Jules. I thought you just had a rabbit."

"No, no, it's not my cat. Technically," Jules says.

"Technically?" David says, scooping up Rover and holding him close to his face.

"Well, this cat was a stray that used to hang out by our house. I mean, I'd been petting him and giving him water, but I hadn't talked my parents into letting me keep him yet." Jules's voice is small, and she looks like she might cry.

"How do you know this is the same cat?" David asks.

Jules starts to answer but nothing comes out. Josh jumps in. "The notch on his ear, the coloring, the dark "M" above his eyes, and that striped tail."

"I got Rover at the animal shelter. He's the cat a bunch of us saw at Stream Cleanup Day. Somebody brought him to the shelter. He had no tags and nobody claimed him. Nobody." David looks at Josh a little angrily, and a little fearfully.

Josh puts up his hands.

"He wasn't our cat, Jules just watched out for him." He looks at Jules as if he is checking to make sure that's true.

Jules nods. Nobody says anything.

And then, Jules puts her arms out to take the cat from David. David's eyes are big, but he lets her take him.

Jules holds Rover up under her chin and rubs Rover on the "M" on his forehead. Rover yawns and rubs his head against Jules's shoulder.

Jules sighs and says, "I'm so glad that Rover finally has a good home. Rover is lucky to have you, David."

I let out the breath I didn't know I was holding.

The door flings open and David's five-year-old sister, Ashley, shouts, "It's time for lunch. Mom said!"

Rover jumps from Jules's arms and runs under the bed.

"You don't have to shout," David tells his sister.

"Sometimes I do," she says. Then Ashley sees

me. "Zoe!" she shouts and hugs me around the waist. "I've been waiting for you for a long, long, long time. I'm so happiest you're back."

"I'm so happiest, too," I say, bending down and giving Ashley a squeeze.

"Ooh, can I wear your necklace?" Ashley fingers my beads. I take them off and put them over her head.

"So sparkly! Okay, come on, it's pizza time!" she shrieks, pulling on my hand and leading me to the kitchen. The rest of the Vet Volunteers follow. My heart starts to race a little, knowing that Brian might be downstairs.

We all find seats at the table. I don't see Brian anywhere, but I pull the lip gloss from my pocket and apply some just in case.

"Napkins in your laps, everyone," Mrs. Hutchinson says, setting the pizza on the table.

Everyone starts noisily passing around the trays of mini pizzas and a bowl of salad. I guess Mrs. Hutchinson figured we needed something healthier than just pizza after all. As I reach for the salad, I see Brian come in. I sit up straighter and flash a big smile at David, hoping that Brian will notice. But he just stands at the kitchen counter, eating pizza with one hand and playing on his phone with the other. I wonder if he's texting some girl. Ashley is beside me, happily chomping on her pizza and swinging her legs playfully.

Then there is a flash and a click. Brenna has taken a picture of her plate.

"What are you doing?" David asks.

"I have a food setting on my camera, and I wanted to try it out," she says, lifting her camera and taking a picture of the salad.

"Food setting?" David repeats. "Do you have a drink setting, too?"

"No, just a food setting," Brenna says, adjusting her lens.

"What about a fool setting?" Maggie asks. "Because that would be Josh and David. You should definitely take a picture with the fool setting."

Brenna points her camera at Josh and David while they make silly faces. Click. I glance over at Mrs. Hutchinson. She doesn't seem upset that this lunch has turned into a loud party. Maybe it's because our napkins are still in our laps.

The kitchen grows noisier as the party continues. Mrs. Hutchinson serves chocolate-chip cookies. They're good, warm, and chewy. I once made cookies like this but used whole-wheat flour, a bit of flaxseed, and some oatmeal. They were delicious, too, but also nutritious. I am about to mention this to Brenna—her family is into healthy eating, too—but then there's a knock on the door. Josh and Jules's dad has come to get them, and the twins introduce me to him.

"Nice to meet you," Mr. Darrow says, shaking my hand. "I expect we'll see you around our place quite a bit. The kids have fixed up our basement as a Vet Volunteers hangout, but I'm sure you've already heard about that. Come on Josh, Jules, let's get moving."

Hmm. I hadn't heard about the hangout, but I haven't really talked to Maggie yet. Josh punches David in the arm as he walks to the door. David grabs him in a headlock. Boys. They can't just say good-bye to their friends.

Jules takes a step outside, then turns around, biting her lip. "David, I'm glad Rover has a real home," she says. "Honest."

"Thanks," David says. It looks like he's going to say something else, but then he just waves at Jules and looks at his feet.

"We ought to get going, too," Brenna says. "You ready, Sunita? Great cat, David!" She snaps a picture of David and heads out the door with Sunita following behind.

I never did get a chance to tell Brenna to take a picture of Brian. Bummer.

I glance around to check out Brian just as he looks my way. Ack! I blush, but Brian smiles and nods. Out of the corner of my eye I see David frown. Now what's up? There's more drama in Ambler today than back in Hollywood.

Chapter Three

• • • • • • • • • • • •

There is no reason to be frightened of tofu," I say, flipping the bean curd over in the pan. Now that I've had two full nights of sleep, my energy is back and I'm cooking an early dinner for my cousin and grandmother. Maggie manages a doubtful smile at my words. Gran looks just as uncomfortable. Really, what do these two eat when I'm not here? Actually, I know the answer to that. They eat frozen dinners and canned soup. Oh, and snack cakes. I've seen the wrappers in the garbage.

Maggie's old basset hound, Sherlock Holmes, is under my feet at the stove. Each time I need something from the refrigerator I have to take a giant step over him. Considering the size of his belly, this is not easy to do. At least Sherlock doesn't seem as suspicious as the two sitting at the table.

Gran looks at the bowl of cranberry-apple chutney I've prepared. "I think I got all the ingredients on your list," she says, "except quinoa. I'm not sure what that is or where I would even find it at Genuardi's." She turns to Maggie and gives her a playful little nudge. "I picked up some Pop-Tarts, too," she whispers. Maggie grins.

"I heard that! You're both going to rot your insides," I say. "All right, I'm all set. Let's eat."

On each plate I spread a little mashed avocado and place a slice of balsamic-fried tofu on top. Then I spoon on the cranberry-apple chutney. It smells wonderful. The sweet and tangy chutney mixes with the nutty scent of the tofu. Mmm, I can't wait to dig in.

Gran sure looks like she can wait, though. She has a strained expression on her face, but then she smiles and takes a tentative bite.

Maggie breathes deeply and says, "It looks so pretty. Kind of Christmasy with all the green and red." She cuts a sliver and puts it on the tip of her tongue.

"Oh for Pete's sake," I say, and take a big bite. Yummm, it is delicious. They'd love it if they'd just give it a chance.

But then the phone rings—the clinic line. Gran jumps up to get it. Maggie looks relieved and puts her fork back down with the sliver of tofu still on it. I frown at her. She shrugs at me.

Behind us Gran is talking fast and asking questions. "How long . . . When . . ." Maggie and I catch snatches of the conversation.

Gran hangs up the phone. "Girls, I need you," she says rushing to the door. Uh-oh. As we scrub up in the Doolittle Room, Gran fills us in.

"We have a four-month-old kitten coming in. The owners report that she is staggering and acting incredibly thirsty. This sounds dire. They've called from their cell so they should be here in moments. Maggie, meet them at the door and hustle them right in here. Zoe, do you remember where we keep the Ringer's IV solution?"

Maggie scoots out of the exam room.

"Sure do," I say, and go to the cupboard to get one clear, sealed plastic bag of Ringer's solution. Gran will use it to replace the kitten's lost fluids. The family said the kitten is thirsty, so I'm sure she's suffering from dehydration, for starters.

I place the bag on Gran's trauma cart. Gran assembles her exam equipment on the sanitized cart and puts her stethoscope around her neck. Just when we've finished preparing everything, I hear a commotion outside, and Maggie is there in an instant with the kitten and her family.

"Her name is Puff," says a little boy who can't even be old enough for kindergarten yet.

His bigger brother and sister look as worried as he does. Their mom is holding back tears. The kitten is well-named. She is a small white puffball of a cat.

"I'm going to try to find out what's wrong with her," Gran says. "It'd be best if you all waited out there while I examine her."

The family heads to the waiting room with Maggie, who will ask questions and pull together any paperwork that might be necessary.

"Any chance Puff ate something she shouldn't have?" Gran calls out.

The mother turns and says, "Not that we know of, but we've just started letting her wander outside. So it's hard to say."

Gran nods, gloves up, and quickly gets to work. I close the door behind the family. The kitten is breathing so fast. I watch as Gran listens to Puff's heart. Gran's brow furrows—this can't be good. The kitten isn't staggering anymore—in fact, she looks unconscious. Gran gently opens Puff's eyes and shines a light into them. The kitten's breath is still coming fast—too fast. And then Puff vomits and seizes. Gran holds her hand out to me, and I know what that means before she even says it. I should give her the Ringer's. But before I can do that, Gran retracts her hand and reaches for the crash cart. This is bad. Very bad. The kitten's heart must have stopped.

Gran shocks the kitten with the defibrillator. She listens to Puff's heart and shocks her again. Nothing. Gran pushes rhythmically on Puff's chest, trying CPR. My heart is beating, and I can feel hot tears fighting to come out. I choke them down, stiffen my jaw, and hold the defibrillator in case Gran needs it again. But no. Gran shakes her head. Puff is gone.

"Let's take a moment," Gran says. I know she means that we'll take a moment before we tell the family. We've done this before, but it doesn't get easier. Gran straightens up and lets out a big sigh. She removes her gloves and I take mine off, too. Then Gran takes off her glasses, wipes her lenses, and then rubs her eyes. She takes a paper sheet from beneath the exam table and places it over Puff. She pats it and says, "Poor Puff, poor girl." Then she nods, and I follow her out of the room. I feel so awful, but I know I have to put on a brave face. This is the hardest part of being a Vet Volunteer.

If there was anyone else in the clinic I know we would take the family into the Herriot Room so they would be alone when we gave them the bad news. But since the clinic is closed, Gran sits down with them in the waiting room. I look at Maggie, and she can tell by looking at our faces that Puff has died. She shakes her head and walks to the counter to grab some tissues as Gran begins to talk.

"I am sorry that I don't have good news. Puff was very sick," Gran begins. I see the older boy sit up quickly and hear his mother take a quick inhale. The younger boy is confused, looking from Gran to his mother and siblings and back again.

"I'm afraid I could not save her," Gran continues. "Puff—"

"She didn't died, did she?" the little boy asks.

"I'm so sorry, but yes, she did," Gran replies. She kneels down so she is eye level with him.

"But you can make her alive again, right? You have the special medicine, right? Mommy told us you had special medicine here," the little boy says. His mother reaches her arm around his waist and pulls him to her. She strokes his hair with her other hand.

"Puff was too sick to get better, unfortunately." Gran looks around at the whole family as she says again, "I'm so sorry."

"But the special medicine . . ." the girl says.

"There wasn't time for special medicine," Gran says. "She was a very sick kitten."

The younger boy is crying loudly into his mother's sleeve. The older boy looks straight ahead and blinks fast. The mom hugs her kids, and I can tell by the way her shoulders shake that she is crying, too. I feel awful for them.

Gran does not rush them. She sits quietly. Maggie hands out tissues to whomever looks like they need one. Maggie looks like she needs one, too. I know I do. I take the one she offers and squeeze her hand for a moment. I sit and watch all of this and seriously wonder why anyone would want to be a vet. Sure, Gran does amazing things—but this part of it is so hard.

After Gran has taken the family in to see Puff and say good-bye, and after the family has gone home, Maggie and I go back to the house. Gran has some work to finish up before she rejoins us.

My cousin and I sit at the kitchen table, moving cold food around our plates. I don't even want to eat now. Maggie sips her water.

"How can you want this?" I ask her.

Maggie, startled, says, "Well, I was willing to try it, but I wouldn't say I exactly *wanted* tofu."

"No, no, not the tofu. This life. How can you want to be a vet like Gran? How can you want to tell people such horrible things about their pets?"

"Because, usually, their pets do get better. They

do. You know that. Usually, we can make them better," Maggie says, tears in her eyes. "Usually."

The phone rings. Maggie gets up to answer.

"Hello? Oh, hi. Mm-hm. Okay, sounds good." She hangs up and turns to me. "That was Gran. She's going to be a while—probably very late. She has to do some tests to figure out why Puff died."

Maggie and I clear the table. I put the cranberry-apple chutney in the refrigerator and scrape most of the tofu into the trash. If my family didn't want to eat this when it was fresh and piping hot, they definitely won't want to eat it now.

"What will Gran eat when she's done?" I ask Maggie.

"Probably cereal. You know how she loves a big bowl of Captain Krispies," Maggie says, wiping the table with a cloth.

I shudder. All that sugar and those artificial ingredients. Yuck. Maggie washes her hands and pulls out the popcorn pot.

"You up for some?" she asks.

"Always," I answer.

Maggie and I don't always agree on everything, but we've never argued over the world's best junk food: popcorn. There's hardly any nutritional value in it, but at least it's all-natural. Sometimes just the smell of popcorn can make you feel better. We could sure use that right now.

I melt butter as Maggie shakes the pan. Soon, the kitchen smells like warm, buttery popcorn. Maggie grabs the overflowing bowl and some napkins. I fix a glass of ice water for myself and snag an orange soda for Maggie. I would never touch soda myself, but after the hard evening we've just had, Maggie deserves her sugary treat. We head to her room and snuggle up on the bed with the popcorn between us. I think it's about time for a cousin catch-up session. Sherlock follows us in and flops down on the floor beside her bed. Soon he is snoring, and everything is starting to feel pretty cozy.

"You know we're glad you're back. Gran and I both are." Maggie bounces her legs a little.

"I'm glad to be back," I say. I'm still not sure I really mean that, but it's nice to know that she wants me here.

Maggie slurps her soda. "Really? I wasn't so sure. You didn't seem too happy when you and Aunt Rose got off the plane." Maggie looks out of the corner of her eye at me as she takes another sip of soda.

I fidget with my water and grab another handful of popcorn.

"Well, it's hard to leave my mom sometimes.

I worry . . ." I stop. I'm not sure I can really trust Maggie with the truth.

"What do you worry about?" Maggie places her soda on her nightstand and swivels to look at me. I hesitate.

"Come on," she says. "Out with it."

"When Mom has an acting job . . . ," I begin— then wait. I don't want Maggie to think badly about my mom. I don't want her to think I'm a baby, either.

"Let's talk about something else," I suggest. "I like your new room color. Did Gran let you paint it yourself?"

"Come on, Zoe," Maggie says. "Don't change the subject." She looks me square in the eye, and I can see that I ought to just spill it.

"When Mom has an acting job," I begin again, "she gets all caught up in it. I think she kind of forgets she has a kid. Nothing in my life can compete with what's going on in hers."

"Why is it a competition?" Maggie asks.

"That's not what I mean. I worry that . . . I worry that . . . I bore her a little." I look to see what Maggie thinks about this.

"Zoe, you couldn't bore anybody." She snatches a pillow and swats me with it. "You're way too much drama, girl."

Maggie is smiling at me, so I take the pillow and whack her on the top of her head with it. Some popcorn falls on the floor. Sherlock wakes from his slumber, lumbers over to where the popcorn fell, and gobbles it down. Nothing like some extra human food to motivate a lazy dog!

Once our mini pillow fight is over, we settle back down and finish off the popcorn. I think about everything that Maggie said. It all makes sense, and maybe Maggie's right. But it still doesn't change the way I feel.

Chapter Four

· · · · · · · · · · · ·

A few days later, Maggie takes me to Wrenches &
Roses. That's the name of Jules and Josh's parents'
business. It's a hardware and gardening store, and
that's where the Vet Volunteers are this morning.
Well, they're in the basement, specifically. Josh
and Jules made it a great hangout space. It's
warmer than a basement usually is, and brighter.
They put a big scrap of lime green carpet on
the floor and moved some giant bookcases
together to partition off their space from the
rest of the basement, which is used for storing
supplies and hosting do-it-yourself workshops
about gardening and home repairs. At one end
of the basement is the rabbit corral and cage for

their rabbit, Cuddles. Or Chewie. I've heard her called both names this morning.

At the other end of the hangout space a Ping-Pong table is set up. David and Josh seem to have commandeered that. A low table the size of a sandbox is in the middle of the room, and lots of colorful beanbag chairs are grouped around it. There are bright lights above us, and somebody must love frogs because frog posters are everywhere. I could have done without those, but all in all, this is an awesome place and it's ours. We could have quite the party down here. Maybe I'll ask Jules if I can organize one for us soon.

Brenna and Sunita play on the floor with Jules's little lop-eared bunny. They're trying to tempt the bunny with some cardboard tubes, but she seems to prefer the odd bit of striped fabric she's carrying around in her mouth. It's like a blankie, and this is weird, but it looks kind of familiar to me. I have no idea why though.

Maggie talks to the boys as they play Ping-Pong. My ears perk up—I think David just said something about his brother. I casually tilt my head toward the boys and Maggie, trying to be cool about it. I definitely don't want Maggie finding out that I kind of like Brian. There'd be no end to the teasing, or worse, the lecturing about him because he's sixteen. I just want to find out more about him. I'd hardly noticed him when I'd lived in Ambler before. But now, well, Brian is interesting.

"He's working at the grocery store three shifts a week," David says, thwacking the ball across the table toward Josh. "Bag Boy Brian. He hates it when I call him that."

Josh taps the ball back at David. "But you call him that anyway?"

"Sure, he calls me names, too. I'm just evening the score." David slaps at the ball and it sails off, way above Josh's head. "If only I was evening the score with you. But no. Too bad. You win. Want to play again?"

Josh laughs. "Maybe, if I can find the ball!" He starts looking for it behind the bookcases. Brenna and Sunita settle into beanbag chairs, and Jules cuddles Cuddles on her lap. I'm leaning awkwardly against one of the bookcases, still not feeling 100 percent at home with the group.

But Brenna reaches up and tugs the hem of my jeans, motioning for me to sit in the beanbag chair next to her.

"Hey, Zoe, Maggie—did Dr. Mac find out what happened to that kitten?" she asks.

"She did," I say. "According to Gran, Puff ingested poison."

"Poison! What kind of poison?" Josh asks worriedly.

"Gran isn't sure yet. The final lab results aren't in," Maggie answers.

"That's horrible! Does she know how Puff was poisoned?" Sunita asks, leaning forward in her beanbag chair.

"Gran will talk to the family again," I say, "after she finds out what the poison was—"

"But she thinks it's an accidental poisoning, right?" Sunita interrupts. She looks like she might cry.

I'm about to answer, but Brenna stops me.

"I've heard about animals being intentionally poisoned. It was in the news last winter. Do you remember, Sunita?"

"Around here?" Sunita asks.

"No, down in Philly," Brenna says. "But that doesn't mean it couldn't happen here. I remember that they caught the guy. He thought it was up to him to fix his neighborhood's stray dog problem. Said he felt justified. The creep."

Then everyone is talking at once. It's possible that someone is poisoning animals. Why are some people cruel to animals? Still, it's more likely that the kitten accidentally got into something she shouldn't have.

I turn to David and ask, "Do you let Rover

outside? Maybe you should keep him in until we know whether this was an accident or if someone in town is poisoning cats."

"Rover goes out with me. I don't let him wander," David says.

"It's hard to keep an outdoor cat from wandering," Sunita warns. "Maybe impossible."

"And Rover was a stray to begin with, don't forget," Jules murmurs.

David looks over at Jules. She smiles tentatively at him. Things seem okay between them, but clearly Jules is worried about Rover.

"I'm going to go get us a snack," Jules says, handing Cuddles to Brenna. "Josh, want to help?" He nods and follows her up the stairs.

But the Rover discussion isn't over. Sunita asks David, "So, how is your little fetching cat?"

David tosses the Ping-Pong ball up in the air and then catches it. Up, down, catch. Up, down, catch. "Well, Rover isn't as much fun as he was at first," he says casually. Up, down, and then David misses the ball and it rolls beneath Cuddles's cage.

"That's not a very nice thing to say," Sunita retorts. She's usually the kindest and sweetest girl in the world, but she sure does get sensitive about cats!

David crawls behind the cage. "Well, it's true.

He sleeps a lot, and he hardly wants to fetch." Still on his knees, David comes out with the ball and tosses it once more. Up, down, catch. "Maybe I should have gotten a dog instead."

"What?" Jules cries as she comes down the stairs, followed by Josh. "How can you say that? Rover is a great cat!"

"I was just telling them that Rover hasn't been as frisky these last few days." David jumps to his feet. "I didn't mean anything by it."

Jules looks shocked. Sunita looks angry.

"David, you are so fickle!" Sunita says. She's standing now, too.

"Fickle, what's that? Some kind of fried pickle?" David jokes.

"That's not funny," Sunita says.

"Maybe Rover is sick," Brenna says from her beanbag chair. We all look down at her. Her brow is furrowed, and she looks like she's been thinking hard. She continues, "Maybe Rover got into whatever that cat Puff got into. Or maybe someone is deliberately poisoning Ambler's cats. Whatever the reason, I think you'd better take Rover to see Dr. Mac."

"Yeah, maybe I better," David says. "But right now I have to babysit Ashley. See you guys later." David takes a handful of cookies from the plate

Josh is holding and heads upstairs. He doesn't look at Jules as he goes by.

Jules stares at Josh. Josh shrugs.

"Well, we've got lemonade, too. Help yourselves," he says, putting the plate and the cups on the low table. Jules sets the lemonade and the napkins down.

Brenna takes a cookie and looks at Jules. "David says stuff like that all the time. He doesn't think when he opens his mouth."

"Sure," Jules says. But she doesn't really look at Brenna. I hardly know Jules, but I can tell she's upset. I check out the lemonade. It looks homemade, so I pour myself some and take a sip. David really needs a pause button on his mouth sometimes.

And Jules isn't the only one who is mad—Sunita is still steaming. Her hands are on her hips, and her mouth is tight. Everyone else in the room is looking down at the ground awkwardly, including me. It seems like we all ought to be going. I think this gathering is over.

Brenna breaks the silence. "Listen, I'll research what I can on that poisoning in Philadelphia and get back to everyone," she says.

"I'll help," I pipe up.

Maggie and I put in a long afternoon cleaning

cages in the clinic. I forgot how much I hate doing this. It's so gross! Maggie doesn't seem to mind at all, whistling as she goes. Gran is nowhere to be seen, but that's okay because there's plenty for us to do. By the time we're done cleaning cages, it's time to feed the kittens again. They all look better, stronger, and even cuter.

It's after nine at night when Gran comes into the clinic to call us to the dinner table. She must be pretty distracted—usually she would never let us go that long without a meal. Maggie and I follow her to the kitchen, where Gran picks up a wooden spoon and starts stirring something in a pot on the stove. She looks concerned, but I have something on my mind, too.

"Gran, did Mom call for me?" I ask, trying to keep the hope in my voice from being too obvious.

"Haven't heard from her. But, Zoe, remember the time difference. Your mother is probably just finishing up work. It's early evening in California."

"Vancouver. She's filming in Vancouver," I say.

"You're right. But it's the same time zone, Zoe," Gran says gently.

I look at the clock. It's nine-twenty here. Six-twenty on the West Coast. Mom's had plenty of time to consider calling her daughter. I've only talked to her once since she left, and that was only for a minute before she got called on set.

Gran taps the spoon on the side of the pot. I get a whiff of its contents. Oh no, canned tomato soup. I need to start cooking again.

Maggie reaches into her backpack and pulls out a bag of gummy bears. "Want some?" she asks me. I shake my head no.

"The lab called tonight. They gave me Puff's results," Gran sighs.

Maggie straightens up and stops chewing her candy.

"Ethylene glycol was in Puff's system. It's what killed her." Gran rubs her forehead. "Such a shame, so preventable." She stirs the soup again.

Maggie lets out a breath. "Ethylene glycol, like Mr. Garcia's dog last December?"

Gran nods.

I have no idea what this ethel whatever stuff is. I want to ask Gran, but she looks a little bit angry. Instead, I look over at Maggie. Maggie looks mad, too. So I just wait it out.

Gran stirs. Maggie scowls. Finally, I stand.

"Okay," I say, "let me at least take over the soup."

Gran concedes and allows me to take the spoon from her. I go to the spice cabinet and find thyme and black pepper and sprinkle them in. Maggie gets bowls and napkins from the cupboard, and she and Gran sit at the table.

I rummage through the refrigerator for the Havarti cheese that I know is in there somewhere. I grab an apple and slice it thin. First the apple slices go on whole-wheat crackers and then the cheese tops them both. I arrange everything on a baking sheet, turn on the broiler, and pop the tray in for a minute. We'll at least have some fruit, protein, and whole grains to go with this canned soup.

I ladle out the soup and put the crackers on a plate on the table. Maggie and Gran eat without saying anything at all. I know them well. They'll talk when they get it all figured out in their heads. I pick up a cracker and take a big bite. Yum, at least something is good tonight. It's warm, sweet, and savory—healthy comfort food. This has to make Gran and Maggie feel a little bit better.

But no one says anything until: "Time for me to head to bed," Gran says, pushing back from the table. "I'll call the family first thing in the morning."

"That's going to be a hard phone call," Maggie says.

"Indeed."

Maggie twists her napkin. Gran crosses her arms over her chest and sighs again. I look from one to the other.

"What?" I can't stand it any longer. "Why will

this be so hard? Their cat is already dead. How could they feel worse?" I ask.

"Because their cat ingested poison," Maggie says.

"I know that."

"Ethylene glycol," Maggie says. "They may have unintentionally poisoned their own cat."

"What? Okay. Will someone please explain to me exactly what ethylene glycol is and where the family would have gotten it?" Honestly, I'm so frustrated I could scream!

Maggie looks at me like I haven't got a brain in my head. "Ethylene glycol. It's most often used as antifreeze for cars. Puff probably licked it up from their own garage floor or driveway."

I look to Gran to see if this is true. She nods and says, "It's dangerous, attractive, and sweet. Even a little can cause death to household pets. Sometimes it drips from the car and puddles on the garage floor or driveway."

Maggie takes the plates and bowls to the sink. "I'm tired," she says. "I'm heading to bed."

Gran nods. She looks tired, too. Then she yelps, "Oh!"

"What?" I can't imagine what Gran has just thought of.

"I can't wait until morning to call. They have young children."

"So, wouldn't they be in bed by now?" I ask and glance at the clock. "I'm sure their mom wouldn't wake them up to tell them how Puff died."

"Children can also be poisoned from antifreeze. Remember, I told you it's sweet. I can't take the chance that those kids are in bed now or that they won't be up early tomorrow. I wouldn't be able to sleep if I didn't call that mother and tell her. She can take a flashlight and look for a leak tonight." Gran goes to the phone and dials. I hear her explaining things to the mother as I run some water in the sink to soak the dishes.

As I'm cleaning up, I start to wonder if I can help in some way. There is a tickling of an idea at the back of my brain. I know if I sleep on it, I'll figure it out. At least, I hope so. I write a few notes to myself about research for tomorrow and tumble into bed, exhausted.

Chapter Five

. . . .

Despite my late bedtime, I'm on the computer researching antifreeze facts before Gran is even up. My thoughts were churning so much, I woke up earlier than usual. There's a ton of information about antifreeze online, but more people need to know about it. I think the Vet Volunteers could be the ones to get the word out to as many people in Ambler as possible. I wonder what the best way to do that would be. I should discuss it with Maggie. Wait—I look at the clock. It's not even six a.m. yet. I better not bother Maggie. She's such a grouch in the morning, and she went to bed late, too. I decide to check my email while I'm waiting. Maybe Mom has written. It's been four days since

she checked in. Not that I'm counting or anything.
She has! I click on the email.
Six lines.

> Hi, Zoe,
> Lots of late nights and early calls here. The
> weather has been interfering with shooting, but
> the week ahead promises to be better. At least
> the cast is fabulous, especially my new friend,
> James. Say hello to Maggie and Mom for me.
> We'll talk soon. Love you!
> Mom

I feel deflated. She didn't even ask anything
about me. I know she knows I'm safe with Gran,
but come on! Isn't she curious to know what I'm
up to? Doesn't she worry about whether or not I'm
happy? And why doesn't she give me more details?
This independent movie in Vancouver should be
the biggest thing that's ever happened to her. Well,
except for having me. She should be telling me
about the production. The set. The costumes. She
should be sharing silly actor gossip with me, not
just telling me she has a friend James. She should
be wishing I was there with her.

I don't hit reply. I'm too angry. I print out my
research notes and turn off the computer. I'll

deal with Mom's less-than-an-email later. First I'll make breakfast for everyone. Quiche. I have a great recipe that uses spinach and low-fat cottage cheese. It's bound to make me feel better, and then I won't have to watch Gran and Maggie chomping on Pop-Tarts.

As I whisk the eggs and chop the spinach, I start to feel a little calmer. While the quiche bakes, I scrub the kitchen until it shines. The sun is streaming in the windows when Gran and Maggie come into the kitchen. Because it's Saturday, the clinic doesn't open until noon today, so we're able to have a relaxing breakfast before Gran needs to run errands.

"That was delicious, Zoe." Gran smiles as I wrap up the leftover quiche. "Now, who wants to help me with my errands?"

"I'll come," Maggie says, looking at me. I pass because I want to think about the antifreeze problem a little more before I bring Maggie and the Vet Volunteers into it all. And I need to decide how to reply to my mother.

"See you in a couple hours," Gran says.

Maggie just waves good-bye, but she acts kind of bouncy, like she might be happy that I'm staying behind. Hmm. Does she want Gran to herself? I suppose that's possible. Now that I'm back, I guess they haven't really had any time without me. I might just be imagining things, but my good mood from breakfast is over.

I go over my notes and research for about an hour more. I still don't know what to say to Mom so I leave that whole issue alone. Instead, I decide to go over to David's house to check on Rover. Maybe Brian will be there, too. That would cheer me up. Plus, I'm looking particularly cute today. I have on my skinniest jeans and my teal chiffon blouse. Mom always says that teal brings out my eyes.

But Brian isn't home. Can't win 'em all.

"I'm babysitting Ashley again," David says as I step inside. "Brian's at work and Mom's shopping. I'm allowed to make peanut-butter-and-jelly cookies. Want some?"

I can't imagine what peanut-butter-and-jelly cookies are, but I say yes because Ashley is standing there grinning and rubbing her tummy like a cartoon character.

"Sure. How long do they take to bake?" I ask. The kitchen is spotless. I can only imagine what kind of mess David will make if he bakes cookies.

"They don't get baked," Ashley says, swinging on the cupboard door. "They get maked."

"Maked, huh?"

"She's right," David says, gently nudging Ashley out of the way so he can reach into the cupboard. He pulls out a jar of peanut butter and a package of vanilla wafer cookies. "They get maked. Er— made."

David finds the jelly in the refrigerator and pulls a butter knife from the drawer. Ashley has a stack of plastic plates in her arms.

"Too many, kiddo," David says. "We just need three."

Ashley puts some of the plates back and leaves maybe four or five on the counter.

David smiles at her and starts spreading peanut butter on some wafers and jelly on others. "Go ahead, do your part," he says to her.

"I make them the best," Ashley says as she squishes the wafers together to form peanut-butter-and-jelly cookies.

They are a little drippy from too much jelly, but otherwise, surprisingly good. David pours us each a glass of milk, and when we're done, he cleans up. I'm impressed. Maybe David has grown up a little since I left.

Full and satisfied, with just a little bit of jelly on her shirt, Ashley skips off to play in her room. It's just David and me now. I got so caught up in the cookies that I almost forgot why I came here in the first place.

"How is Rover?" I ask.

"About the same. Come see." David leads the way to his room. Rover is curled up on David's bed. He doesn't react when David pets him.

"Poor Rover," I whisper. "You didn't bring him to the clinic, did you?" I probably would have noticed if he had, but maybe they came when I was out of the house.

"Not yet. He started looking better, but then he went back to being lethargic."

"Gran should be back by now. Don't you think you ought to have her take a peek?"

"Maybe." David looks uneasy.

I don't want to worry him too much, but this is important. "We got Puff's results back. It turns out she was poisoned by antifreeze. Maybe that's not what's happening to Rover, but it would be better to figure it out sooner rather than later." I watch David's face. He lowers his head. His shaggy bangs hide his eyes.

"Okay, let's take him in," he agrees.

I go to pick up Rover, but he slinks away. He moves toward the door. I don't want to scare him so I follow slowly. But he keeps on moving right out the door and down the hall.

"Sorry," I say to David. I wish Sunita or Jules was here. I'm much better with dogs than I am with cats. We watch as Rover disappears into Ashley's room.

"Hi, Rover, wanna play dress up?" we hear her ask.

"No, Ashley!" David calls. "Don't you dare. He might be sick."

We go to her door. Ashley is on the floor, surrounded by her dolls and stuffed animals.

"I can't anyway," she says. "He's under my bed."

And that's where he stays—as far away as possible—way beneath the farthest corner of Ashley's bed. Did I scare Rover? I was just trying to help him.

David and I sit on the floor beside Ashley's bed, amongst all of her stuffed friends, and try to figure out what to do.

"I don't think we ought to reach in there," I say, lifting the bedspread and looking under the bed. "He's backed himself into the corner and his fur is bristly. He looks afraid enough to bite."

"Okay, we'll leave him alone for a bit," David says, and I let the bedspread fall back.

Ashley gives me a teacup and a cookie, both made of plastic. Next she hands the same to David. He quickly puts his on her floor like he doesn't know what to do with them.

"No, David, do it the way you're supposed to," Ashley chastises.

Supposed to? Sounds like they've done this before. David blushes. I bet he doesn't want me to know he plays tea party with his sister. He takes a small, pretend sip.

"Come on, the right way!" Ashley says. "The right way," she repeats.

David holds the teacup in one hand and extends his pinky. Oh my gosh, he *has* done this before. He takes a sip and makes a teensy, almost proper, sipping sound. With his other hand, he takes the fake cookie and dunks it daintily into the plastic teacup and then . . . he gobbles, gobbles, gobbles as loud as he can, just like Cookie Monster.

"Cookie, cookie, cookie!" he growls.

Ashley falls over laughing. "That's the right way!" she says. I can tell this is a favorite game for both of them.

"Nice work, Hutchinson, nice work," I say. David blushes. I pretend not to notice and gobble my cookie, too. I'm not as loud as David, but Ashley still laughs.

"You're not going to mention this to any of the guys at school, are you?" he asks.

"Wouldn't dream of it," I say.

That's when we notice that Rover is panting. From beneath the bed, his breathing is quick and fairly loud. David looks under the bed, clicks his tongue, and calls softly, "Come on, Rover, nck, nck, nck." I can tell that he's alarmed but that he doesn't want to upset Ashley.

"You sound like you're trying to get a horse's attention," I say. "Try this: Ppsss, ppsss, ppsss." I wiggle my fingers at Rover.

Rover looks at us but stays put.

My mind is racing. Rover doesn't look like he's in really bad shape like Puff did, but I really want to get him to the clinic. "Maybe we can move the bed away from the wall and you can reach him," I suggest.

"You can use my stuffed animals like a fence so he can't get by," Ashley suggests. "If you use the biggest ones it should work."

"Great idea," David says. "Of course, if Rover actually felt fine, a fence of stuffed animals wouldn't be anything to him. He'd sail right through."

But the way Rover looks now he's unlikely to even hop over Ashley's Barbie dolls. Ashley and I gather up all the dolls and stuffed animals from the floor. She lays on her stomach and scoots halfway under the bed. David hands her the toys one by one to build the fence.

"Get the pet carrier before we move the bed," I say. "Then we can tuck him right into it." David nods and goes to fetch the carrier from downstairs.

Ashley and I finish setting up the stuffed-animal fence. It begins under the bed and makes a path for Rover to follow.

David returns with the carrier and closes the door behind him. "So he doesn't escape," he explains.

I guide Ashley away from the bed. "Stay beside me while David gets Rover, okay?" Ashley's eyes are huge, but she just nods and holds the carrier, open and ready. David gets into position to move the bed. I'm crouched down with my hands ready to scoop Rover up as soon as he does. I sure hope this works.

David counts, "One . . . two . . . three . . ." and he lifts. Rover is curled into a tight ball. The cat gets to his feet and looks around, but he's stopped by the stuffed animals. I bend down and pick him up before he can figure out what's going on. Ashley holds the carrier door open and I slip Rover in.

"Whew. No problem at all." David looks relieved.

"Let's head over," I say.

"Can I come? Can I come?" Ashley begs.

"We couldn't have done it without you. You'd better come," David says. Then he turns to me and whispers, "I'm babysitting, she has to come."

True, there is nobody to stay with her here. Mrs. Hutchinson is still gone, and Brian hasn't showed up, either. Looks like I wasted one of my best outfits on a tea party and a cat rescue.

Chapter Six

• • • • • • • • • • • •

In the Dolittle Room, Gran checks Rover all over.
She listens to his heartbeat and breathing with
her stethoscope. Rover sleeps through this part.
Gran gently feels every inch of him. I know she
is checking his skeleton and also checking for any
odd lumps or bumps he might have. She checks
his reflexes, which wakes him up. The tapping
of Gran's tiny rubber hammer must be hard to
ignore. She looks in Rover's ears, eyes, and mouth
with her scope. She's checking for mites and signs
of infection.

"Will he be all right?" David asks worriedly. "Did
his heart sound okay? His reflexes worked, right?"

I put my hand on David's elbow. He takes a deep

breath and stops asking questions. With my other hand, I squeeze Ashley's shoulder. She's being surprisingly quiet and well-behaved during the exam. Maybe doctor's offices make her nervous.

Gran continues her exam. She listens to Rover's lungs and heart again.

"I'm not sure what is making Rover so sluggish." Gran flips her stethoscope back up around her neck. "I'm going to do some blood work to see if I can get some answers. I'd like to keep Rover overnight so I can keep an eye on him."

David looks pale. "Do you think it's serious?"

"When an animal suddenly becomes lethargic—that is cause for concern. Animals slow down as they age, just like people do. But Rover isn't very old, so sudden changes in behavior absolutely need to be checked out." Gran pats David on the shoulder.

"What about antifreeze? Zoe said that kitten died from it."

"I'm including that test in the blood work."

I wish I could make David feel better. I turn to him and say reassuringly, "So it's good you brought him in, then." He looks at me and half-smiles.

Gran picks up Rover. "David, do you want me to call your mother, or can you convey this all to her?"

"I'll tell her. It's fine." David scratches Rover under his chin, waves to me, and leaves the exam room. I see Ashley take David's hand as they walk out of the clinic.

Before we can finish sanitizing the exam room, we have an emergency. Seconds after we hear the jingle of the door and panicked voices, we rush out to reception. It's a dog, vomiting and making a horrible crying sound. Gran passes Rover off to me. "Cage six, far from the kittens," she says, turning to this new dog and taking him into the Herriot Room. I hear her send his family into the waiting room.

I quickly put Rover in his cage, making sure to tuck a warm towel in with him. It'll keep him warm and should comfort him, too. I latch the door and head quickly to the Herriot Room.

The dog is beautiful—or should be. He's a chocolate Lab with short deep-brown hair, and he must weigh about a hundred pounds. But he looks so weak. Luckily, Gran is the best vet around here, so he's in good hands now.

Gran is listening to the dog's breathing and heartbeat. "Call Maggie to help with the family," she instructs.

"Do you want me to get their information?"

"No, I need you here. Call Maggie," Gran says

without looking up from the poor animal. I'm totally focused on the dog, but I can't help thinking that it's nice to feel needed.

I call our home line from the clinic phone. Before I can get back to Gran, Maggie is rushing in to work with the family. She'll get the dog's health history and more information on what happened before they brought him here.

Back in the Herriot Room, things look bad. The dog is still throwing up. Yuck, I will never get used to that. I whisk away the gross cloths and replace them with clean ones. I stand back, wondering what else I can do. But I know not to ask questions, that Gran will let me know what she needs.

Maggie scoots in the room. "Three-year-old Lab. Been throwing up for a few hours. They said he looked drunk earlier. They imagined it was just something he ate. But he started crying about a half hour ago and walking stiffly so they decided to bring him in. Oh, his name's Jinx. Do you want me to get his dad?"

"Yes," Gran says, "this is a very sick dog."

"Reminds me of Puff," I say.

Gran and Maggie nod. Gran begins an IV, and Maggie leaves to get the dog's owner.

"Okay, Jinx," Gran coos to the dog, petting his neck. "Let's find out why it all hurts so much."

An hour later, Gran has stabilized Jinx. She lets us have a break while she talks to the dog's family, so my cousin and I head to the kitchen. Saving animals makes you hungry!

Maggie pulls out the box of Pop-Tarts. "Want one?" she asks, taunting me.

"Sure," I say. Maggie is surprised. So am I. Curiosity has gotten the better of me, I suppose. How bad can they be? And Maggie loves them. It would be nice to share something with my cousin other than popcorn.

The toaster springs up two lightly browned rectangles. Maggie hands me one wrapped in a napkin, warm and smelling of strawberry. It's frosted and covered in red and pink sprinkles. I'm sure it doesn't need all that extra sugar to top it off, but it does look pretty. Maggie pours us each a small glass of milk and flops down in the chair opposite me.

"Oh come on, take a bite," she says, and chomps a mouthful. I nibble the corner. It doesn't taste like much. I take a bigger bite and the warm strawberry filling oozes pleasantly into my mouth. Uh-oh. It's delicious. Now I know why Maggie and Gran are hooked on these things.

"It's . . . not bad," I lie.

Maggie raises her eyebrows and gets up and

puts two more Tarts in the toaster. She sits back down and starts spinning her empty glass of milk on the table.

"So what do you know about your mom's movie?" she says, looking at her glass, not directly at me.

"It's an independent film with a small budget but some big stars," I reply. I've gotten so used to people asking this question, the response comes automatically.

"Is your mom one of the big stars?" Maggie stops spinning her glass and looks up.

"Not even close. But she hopes this movie will get her closer to becoming one."

"Gran really hasn't told me about it. I have the feeling she knows practically nothing about what's going on."

"I know practically nothing, too," I say, a little sullenly. Then I reconsider. "Well, maybe that's not entirely true." I take a sip of my milk and continue. "It's a trilogy. I overheard her talking to her agent about the filming schedule. If the financial backing comes through, they'll film the three movies one after the other without a break."

Maggie hands me another Pop-Tart and refills our glasses. "So what else is there to know, then?"

I take a big sip of milk and choke on it a little.

"My mother hasn't told me any of this. If I hadn't overheard her conversation I'd assume I was just here for the rest of the school year. And maybe I am; who knows? But then there's summer, and she said I can visit on set then. Visit, because I'm living here? Or visit from some apartment Mom and I are sharing in Vancouver?"

I bang my glass down, and a little milk splashes up and onto the table.

"Oops," I say.

Maggie jumps up from her chair and says, "Lemme get it." She starts wiping the table with the dishcloth and nods for me to continue.

I start toying with my napkin. "Filming is stressful for Mom. She loves it, you know? But as time goes by, she becomes less and less of a mom and more of . . . well, a distracted and messy roommate."

Maggie nods. "I guess that's why it's good that you're here."

"But for how long? Wouldn't it be nice to know at least that?"

"Just ask her," she says. "Just ask your mom how long she thinks you'll be here. And if she doesn't know, ask her when she will know."

"You don't understand—"

"Listen, Gran is great, but if I *had* a mom, I

know I would talk to her about important things."

I shake my head. "Mom—"

Maggie interrupts again. "Your mom is fun, funny, and bighearted—but she is impulsive. And you? You're stubborn, like me, I guess. What can it hurt to ask her directly?" She sighs and turns away.

I don't know. I guess Maggie's right. I have a right to know how long I'll be in Ambler. If Mom gets mad that I'm asking, at least there are three thousand miles between us. She really can't punish me from Vancouver. What can it hurt?

I look over at my cousin. She's petting Sherlock, who has wandered in from another room. I realize that as frustrating as my mom can be to deal with, I should be grateful that I have her. Maggie's parents died in a car crash when she was a baby. All she has is Gran. A great veterinarian, a wonderful grandmother, but still, Gran is not Maggie's mother. I've heard Maggie tell people that Gran is a great mom *and* a great dad. But Maggie doesn't really know what it's like to have a mom who was her own age not so long ago. A mom who knows the latest fashions. A mom who knows which bands are cool and which magazines to buy. A mom like mine, when I have her.

We finish our Pop-Tarts in silence. Sherlock settles his big old self beneath Maggie's chair.

Soon, he is huffing and snoring away.

I decide we need to have a big salad for supper after all that sugar and fat. Maggie pulls out the homework she's been putting off during spring break. She sits down at the kitchen table and huffs just like Sherlock. Bored already, I guess. Maggie has never liked schoolwork all that much.

I chop vegetables and think about school starting up on Monday. Just two days away. School in Ambler, Pennsylvania, again. And for how long? Most likely I'll finish out the year here. Will I start school again in the fall with Maggie, or will I be back with my friends in California? Will I be here a couple of years? I chop the celery so hard, Maggie looks up from her math.

"Need help with that stuff?" she asks.

"This 'stuff' is celery, and no, I don't," I say. "I'll let you know when supper's ready."

Maggie goes back to her books, and I fling the chopped celery into the bowl of lettuce. I peel and shred some carrots and feel my shoulders relax a little. Carefully, I slice tomatoes and sweet red peppers. Soon I have assembled a beautiful, colorful bowl of vegetables. I might not have any answers about the future, but I feel much calmer knowing that soon I'm going to pin Mom down with my questions.

Maggie and I eat by ourselves because Gran hasn't returned from the clinic. My cousin doesn't even complain about the salad. Maybe my Pop-Tart peace treaty did the trick.

Much later, Gran finally comes home. Maggie and I have waited up for her in the kitchen. Well, I've waited up. Maggie is asleep on top of her homework. My mind is racing with thoughts of Jinx and Rover.

Gran pats her on the shoulder as she goes by and wearily says, "I need a shower, and you girls ought to be in bed. I think Jinx has turned the corner."

Maggie wakes, startled. "Do you know what's wrong with him?" she asks, rubbing her eyes.

"I suspect ethylene glycol," Gran says, and heads to her room.

"Again?!" I look at Maggie.

"It's terrible!" Maggie shakes her head.

"This can't be a coincidence. We need to find out where the antifreeze is coming from, and whether it's deliberate or accidental." I stand and stretch.

Maggie nods. "The other Vet Volunteers don't even know that it's antifreeze yet. We ought to get everyone together tomorrow and brainstorm."

Well, David knows. But somehow I don't feel like telling my cousin that David and I spent time together today. Maggie knows me pretty well, and I don't want her guessing that I went over to the Hutchinsons' hoping to see Brian. Instead, I suggest that we start brainstorming tonight.

"I've actually been working on this already if you want to take a look before tomorrow—"

"You have? That's great, Zoe! But I'm sorry, I can't stay up any longer," Maggie says. "I promise we can work on it tomorrow. G'night."

I'm tired, too, but tonight's news has me even more determined to get things going. I rummage through the junk drawer until I find construction paper and markers. I have plenty of work to do tonight. But first, I call my mom on her cell phone. It goes straight to voicemail, so I leave a message and turn to my computer. I send one email to the Vet Volunteers about the meeting and another to my mother about my life. I tell her about Jinx and Rover, and how cool the Wrenches and Roses hangout is. I'll save my big questions for when we talk on the phone.

Once that's done, I work for another couple of hours on the computer, checking every now and then to see if Mom has responded to my email. Between flips over to my email account, I've managed to set up a simple website for the Vet Volunteers. We can use it for a lot of things, but my first idea is to create short video public service announcements, or PSAs, and post them on the site. I'm sure the other kids will be excited to act in them. We can give valuable information to the public about all kinds of animal care, starting with antifreeze dangers. I can direct—I've been on set enough times to pick up some tips. And Mom has always told me I'm a natural actress, just like her, so I can show the other Vet Volunteers how it's done. I won't even tell my mother about it. Once we're done, I'll just send her a link to the site. I bet she'll be really proud of me when she sees me following in her footsteps and helping animals. It might even make her miss me more.

I check one last time to see if Mom has answered my email. Still nothing. She hasn't returned my phone call, either. My heart sinks. I shut everything down and go to bed.

Chapter Seven

• • • • • • • • • • •

The next day, the Vet Volunteers meet at Wrenches
& Roses. Mrs. Darrow has left a plate of veggies and
dip for us. Once we're all settled in our beanbags—
and Cuddles is hopping all over that lime-green
carpet—I try to get everyone's attention.

"Ahem," I say, clearing my throat and waving
my arms.

No one pays attention. "Uh-hmmm!" I say
again, even louder.

Sunita notices and nudges Brenna. The boys
keep talking. "Uh-hmmm," I repeat, and kick
David in the shin.

"Hey! Whadja do that for?" he says, rubbing
his leg.

Oh, come on. He's being dramatic. I didn't kick him hard. It was really more of a strong nudge. At least now everyone is quiet and paying attention to me.

"Okay, guys. I have an announcement." I speak slowly so they will understand how important this is. I am wearing my most serious outfit: black turtleneck, black jeans, and a teal scarf for a little pop of color. It makes me feel very artistic.

I take a deep breath and say, "We need to discuss antifreeze."

No one says anything.

"We sell antifreeze," Josh says. "Do you need some? I can run up and ask my dad for a gallon." He rises from his chair. Maggie shakes her head, and Josh sits back down.

"No," Maggie says. "We don't need any. Antifreeze poisoning is what Puff died from. And we had a very sick dog in the clinic last night, and Gran says he has antifreeze poisoning, too. She still isn't sure if he's going to make it."

Argh, she just blurted it all out! I was building up to the explanation for dramatic effect. I was going to tell them all the details as soon as I knew I had everyone's attention.

Sunita's eyes grow wide.

"So you think there could be someone

intentionally poisoning animals? Or maybe there's an antifreeze leak somewhere?" she asks.

"Well, we don't know for sure, of course. But with two cases of antifreeze poisoning, we should start looking into both," I reply.

"We've had a report of dead raccoons, a whole family of them," Brenna says. Her family runs a wildlife rehabilitation center. "I wonder if it could be related. I'd better call my folks." Brenna gets up and dials her cell. I watch her move to the Ping-Pong table end of the basement to talk quietly.

"So the way I see it, we have a two-part project ahead of us." I look at the Vet Volunteers one by one to be sure that everyone is ready to hear this. Good. We're all focused today. I motion to Maggie to hold up my construction paper posters.

Brenna is off the phone and settled again in her chair. I point to the first poster.

"This is antifreeze—"

"Or ethylene glycol," Maggie interrupts.

"Or ethylene glycol," I continue. "Sometimes it's called engine coolant, too. Anyway, we'll just refer to it as antifreeze. This is what it looks like."

The Vet Volunteers lean forward in their chairs

to see the picture I've printed from the Internet.

My six facts are printed on the posters, but I know that it will have more impact if I also recite them to the group. So I begin:

> "Antifreeze is a bright yellow or bright green liquid with a slightly sweet smell and taste.
>
> Antifreeze is used in the radiators of cars, trucks, and other motor vehicles, like boats and RVs, to keep them from overheating in the summer or freezing in the winter.
>
> Antifreeze can leak out of vehicles when radiators and cooling lines are damaged.
>
> People may spill antifreeze if they don't pour carefully.
>
> Spilled and leaked antifreeze is appealing to animals and young children because of its color, its smell, and its sweet taste."

I take a big breath. "This is our most important fact:

> Antifreeze is a powerful poison, so sipping or just licking it can kill an animal or a small child."

I look around at a speechless Vet Volunteers group. And then, everyone seems to talk at once. Josh remembers hearing about antifreeze poisoning at his old school in Pittsburgh; Sunita asks about symptoms; Brenna takes notes. Cuddles hops around under the table, then stands on her hind legs to see what is up there. Jules plucks a carrot stick from the plate and gives it to her. Cuddles goes to work on her treat.

"Everyone? Everyone?" I need them to focus so they can hear the rest of my plan. Once they've settled again, I take another deep breath and tell them the exciting part.

"I think we need to design a public awareness campaign about the dangers of antifreeze," I say.

"But first we should try to find out if these poisonings are accidental or intentional," Brenna says. "We need to find out where the antifreeze is coming from before more animals die!"

"Or kids!" David says. "Just look at Zoe's list; kids can die from it, too."

I jump back in. "Well, yeah, I already thought of that. This brings me to my second poster." Gosh, they sure know how to mess up an orchestrated moment. I'll explain the PSAs to them later, I guess.

I point to the second poster that Maggie holds.

"We need to find out if any other vets around Ambler have treated animals with antifreeze poisoning. We need to check with the wildlife rehab." I nod at Brenna. "And we ought to check with state-park rangers, too."

Jules adds, "Let's not forget the animal shelter. There are a couple vets on staff there and they may have noticed something."

"Perfect!" Brenna says. "We may be able to find a geographic center for these cases."

David looks confused. "Huh?"

Brenna has taken over. "By talking to wildlife specialists and vets who have treated sick pets, we can map where these animals have been. Then we can find the source of the antifreeze."

"And if we can find it, then we can clean it up and prevent other animals and children from finding it," Sunita chimes in.

"Exactly!" I am happy that everyone gets my plan, but I had a really exciting ending for my presentation. I was going to dramatically introduce my PSA idea by pretending that I'm an announcer on television. Oh well. No reason to bother with it now; everyone is already dividing up the duties.

Brenna and Jules will contact the state-park rangers and Brenna's own parents. Jules will also call the animal shelter. Sunita and Maggie will talk to Gran and the other vets around Ambler. Josh and David will get a map and chart where the sick animals have been.

"And what will you be doing?" David asks me.

"I will be compiling all of our results and working on details of the PSAs."

"What PSAs?" Brenna asks.

"Well, I was going to go over that now. But I think I'll wait until we get a handle on finding the source of the antifreeze," I say, looking around the room. "I can tell you the PSA part will be exciting, and it will involve all of us." And maybe even get my mother interested in my life again.

David looks at Josh and shrugs. Brenna shakes her head and pulls out her phone.

I hear Sunita whisper to Maggie, "Do you know what she's planning?"

"No idea," Maggie answers.

Good. I've managed to maintain a little drama.

We begin our research right away. I watch as the Vet Volunteers pair up, sharing clipboards and paper. Josh and David go upstairs to see if the store has an area map. Everyone is getting down to business, so I pull out my pad and start writing out my ideas for the first PSA.

We've only been working for about ten minutes when Josh and David return with a rolled-up map and a big corkboard. Josh leans the corkboard against one of the big bookcases and David pins the map up. Brenna, still on the phone, walks over to the map. Jules carries her clipboard over to Josh. From where I'm sitting, I see him look at what Jules has written and poke a few colored pins into the map. David wraps colored string around the pins. Interesting. That must be a region they found sick animals in.

I can hear Maggie talking with Gran. Sunita takes notes as Maggie repeats what Gran is telling her. This is going to work, I can tell!

Two hours later, we have nine pins on the map, indicating reported cases of antifreeze poisoning. Five are for pets, including Jinx, and four are for wild animals that have been diagnosed with, or are assumed to have, antifreeze poisoning. David and Josh stretch the string between the pinpoints, creating a circle. The Vet Volunteers huddle around the map.

"X marks the spot!" David says, pointing.

"Hey, that's not far from my house!" Brenna exclaims, peering at the map. "It's close to where the stream empties into Beltzville Lake."

I point to a blue pin. "Look at this. Puff lived right here at the lakeshore. She's the closest pin to the water."

"She was the first fatality that we know of, right?" Josh asks.

I nod. The other cases include three dogs, two cats, a raccoon family, and a red fox. So sad. We couldn't help Puff or the others who have died, but maybe we can make it safe for the rest of the animals in Ambler.

Sunita looks at David. "How is Rover doing?"

"Dr. Mac is taking care of him. Trying to figure out what's up." David doesn't meet her eyes.

Jules leans in. "Does Dr. Mac think it's antifreeze with him, too?"

"She doesn't know yet," David says, finally looking up. "We'll see."

The talk of Rover makes me remember how crucial our timing is. I stand up. "We need to get going."

"Where?" Jules asks.

"Right here." Maggie points to the area of the map that the strings converged on. "We'll look for spilled antifreeze."

"We can have some adults drive us over," Sunita suggests.

"I'm on it," Brenna says, pulling out her phone once more.

A few minutes later, we have a plan. Brenna's dad will pick up four of us, and Mr. Darrow will take the rest of us over to Beltzville Lake. We gather up our clipboards and paper. Josh decides to bring the map and corkboard because they will fit in his dad's van.

When Brenna's dad arrives, he has some bad news for us. A couple of sick great blue herons have been brought to him, and he thinks it could be the antifreeze again. We have no time to lose.

At the lake we divide into two groups. My group consists of Jules, me, David, and Mr. Darrow. Brenna, Josh, Sunita, Maggie, and Mr. Lake are in the other group.

Mr. Darrow has brought flashlights from Wrenches & Roses, and he hands them out to a few of us in each group. "I know it's light out, but these might help detect the liquid's sheen," he says.

The air is warm for April, and people are relaxing at the lake. Lots of people have brought along their dogs and kids to enjoy the day. I see a group of teenagers fishing and a golden retriever paddling near the lake's edge. Nearby, a girl tosses a Frisbee to her cocker spaniel. He runs, leaps, and gracefully catches it. I wonder if we should warn anyone. But no, we don't want to make people panic. We should just try to find the antifreeze as fast as possible.

First, we scour the huge parking lot. Spilled

antifreeze seems likely to be where cars usually are. We shine our flashlights around the empty spaces, hoping to pick up some sheen from the antifreeze. The flashlights are also helpful for looking beneath the cars parked around the lot. It's a good thing Mr. Darrow thought to bring them.

Unfortunately, though, the flashlights don't turn up any antifreeze. After a half hour of searching, we've found nothing. We decide to move closer to the lake.

We spread out to cover more space and step carefully as we search the ground. We sweep our flashlights from side to side. My group moves east from the parking lot toward the boat launch along the shoreline. The other group will move west along the shoreline from the parking lot toward the playground. If we don't find anything on that pass, we'll move farther from the shore and search again.

"What's this?" David asks, investigating a patch of wet ground beside a storage shed.

"There's no sheen to it," Jules says, passing her flashlight's beam across it.

We trace a trail of wet earth back to a dripping faucet on the far side of the shed.

"Just water," David sighs.

Mr. Darrow turns the faucet tight to the right

and the drip stops. If only we could stop the anti-freeze leak just as easily.

"At least we've stopped some water waste," I say to David. He looks disappointed.

We scan the beach to see where the other group is. They're pretty close to the playground, and it's easy to tell by their methodical walk that they haven't found anything yet, either. I'm starting to feel discouraged. I wonder if we will turn up anything at all. Back at Wrenches & Roses this had seemed like such a good plan.

"Once we get to the boat launch, will we start another pass?" David looks at me.

I nod.

But it turns out we don't have to make a second pass, because as we near the boat launch we see two things. One: a big black dog. Two: the big, shiny neon-green puddle he's sniffing.

Chapter Eight

• • • • • • • • • • •

Don't shout, whatever you do!" David says in a low voice. "We don't want to scare him. If he's a stray, we might lose him."

He's right, but it's so hard not to run right at the dog. What if he drinks the antifreeze? Mr. Darrow motions that he will go around the boat launch on the shore side. Jules follows and quickly peels off to move to the far side of the dog. David and I are coming up in front of the dog. Hopefully this won't give him any opportunity to get past us.

We all approach the dog quickly but quietly. The puddle is fluorescent green and so bright that it almost glows. Then I hear a voice coming from right beside me.

"Hey, boy, sit!"

The dog sits.

"Come!"

What? It's David, calling the dog. David, who told us not to shout!

I stare at David, but his eyes are trained on the dog, who doesn't move. He cocks his big black head to the side and stays sitting. He opens his mouth and his big red tongue hangs out.

David kneels down and slaps his thighs. "Hey, boy, come," he repeats.

The dog looks back at the antifreeze but trots right over to David.

"Good boy, good fella," David coos, scratching the dog's neck.

Yes! We've got him. "How did you know he wouldn't get scared?" I wonder.

"I noticed that he has tags on, so he must be somebody's pet. I figured he would know commands, so I took a chance," is all David says. Jules and Mr. Darrow hurry over to us.

"Well done, David," Mr. Darrow says.

"I wonder if his owner is anywhere around?" Jules asks, scanning the lakeshore.

"More importantly, has he licked up any of that antifreeze?" I ask.

We look closely at the dog. He's wet all

over—from the lake, no doubt—so it's hard to tell if his muzzle is wet from the antifreeze or from water. His dark coloring makes it especially difficult.

"I think we'd better let Dr. Mac take a look, just to be safe," Mr. Darrow says. David turns around and whistles for the other group.

As soon as everyone else arrives, we fill them in on what happened. Maggie immediately bends down to pet the dog.

"Oh, boy, good, good, boy, you don't mind if I take a look, do you?" Maggie croons to the dog. I'm not sure what she's thinking when she takes a tissue from her pocket. She quickly wipes his muzzle and shows us the damp tissue. Uh-oh. It's stained a yellowish green.

Maggie straightens up. "I don't know if he ingested any of this, but he definitely sniffed it and touched it with his mouth."

"Great thinking, Maggie," Mr. Darrow says.

"Your experience shows," Mr. Lake adds.

Maggie and David both knew what to do with the dog. I'm a little disappointed that I didn't. But, I did figure out this plan in the first place. And I just know everyone will be excited about the PSAs. I can feel it.

Maggie reaches down and checks the dog's tags.

"His name is Jet," she informs us. "You're a good boy, Jet!" She ruffles the fur around his collar.

Mr. Darrow takes a look at the phone number on the tags and calls Jet's owner. He explains what happened. Apparently Jet got away when his owner, Mr. Jenkins, took his leash off to let Jet roam. He's on the other side of the park, so Mr. Darrow gets permission to bring Jet in to Gran, and Mr. Jenkins will meet us there. And it turns out that Jet is a patient at Dr. Mac's Place anyway.

Once Mr. Darrow gets off the phone, he turns to the group.

"While I'm with Jet at Dr. Mac's, the rest of you kids can help by cleaning up that antifreeze spill. I have rubber gloves in the van and you'll all need to wear them and be very careful. Antifreeze can be absorbed through the skin."

Mr. Lake nods his head in agreement. "I'll supervise, and then I'll call the authorities to let them know what we found."

"Sounds like a plan," Mr. Darrow replies. "David, Zoe, would you like to come with me? Jet seems to be comfortable around you two."

"Sure!" we say in unison, and hop in the van.

On the way to the clinic, I compliment David again on his quick thinking with the commands. "He might have run from us if you hadn't thought of making him sit."

David smiles.

We're in the backseat of the van with Jet on the floor between us. The dog doesn't seem to mind the car ride.

David rubs Jet's wet neck. "Well, for a while I had plenty of experience with practicing doggie commands on my cat." He furrows his brow and turns toward the window. Even if he won't let me see his face, I know that he's hurting.

"We'll be at the clinic soon. Maybe Gran has some answers for you," I say. I pet Jet and hope, hope, hope, that both this dog and Rover will be fine.

Mr. Jenkins is already at the clinic when we arrive. Gran takes him and the dog into the Herriot Room.

"Need me?" I ask my grandmother.

"I'll call if I do. Clean the kittens' cage, won't you?"

I go back into the recovery room to work with the kittens. In a month or so, they should be ready for homes. Gran says they're all getting stronger. Even the little calico looks good.

David follows me but doesn't help with the kittens—not that I need him to. He doesn't joke, doesn't talk. He just opens Rover's cage and pets his cat gently. Rover is still not himself, and neither is David. I turn my attention to the meows beside me.

My friend and I spend the next twenty minutes in silence, as I clean the cage and David keeps Rover company.

Eventually, Gran brings Jet back to the recovery room.

"We'll keep him overnight for observation," she says. "I can't be sure yet if he actually ingested the antifreeze or if he was only curious enough to get it on his muzzle."

I see that Gran has inserted an IV into Jet's front paw. She notices me looking at it and explains, "This will help if he did get some of the antifreeze, and it won't hurt if he didn't." Jet doesn't seem to mind. He's looking sleepy. Gran must have given him an anesthetic in the Herriot Room.

After Gran puts Jet in one of the big dog cages, she talks quietly to David and then leaves to do some paperwork in the office. I couldn't hear what they said, but I don't think I'll ask David, either. He doesn't look terribly conversational yet. I'm long finished with the kittens' cage, and it's not quite time to feed them. But I stay with David in case he wants company.

The rest of the Vet Volunteers return from the

lake about an hour later. They wander back into the recovery room.

"So what's up with Jet?" Josh asks.

David speaks up. "Dr. Mac isn't sure if he actually drank any antifreeze. She's keeping him for observation."

"And how is Rover?" Josh asks David.

"Still lethargic. Dr. Mac has done blood tests, a stool sample, and she's checked enzymes. It doesn't look like antifreeze poisoning—"

"That's a relief!" Sunita interrupts.

"But we still don't know what's wrong with him," David continues. He closes Rover's cage and walks dejectedly out of the room.

Nobody says anything. Maggie checks the hanging chart on the kittens' cage.

"I cleaned their cage," I tell her. "I don't think I marked it off, though."

Maggie checks the box on their chart that I should have. Brenna pets a sleeping Jet through his cage door.

"Almost done with these guys," Maggie says to Sunita as they prepare the kittens' bottles.

"What's happening with them?" I ask.

Sunita smiles and answers happily, "They're doing great! We have homes lined up for all five, once they're old enough to be adopted."

She tests the temperature of the formula and scoops up a kitten.

Josh says, "That's great news. At least we know we'll have a happy ending with them." He leaves. I wonder if he is going to find David.

But right now what I really want to know is more about the antifreeze puddle. "Any thoughts on how that antifreeze got to the lake?" I look at the others.

Sunita nods. "Brenna's dad has a pretty good idea of what happened. It makes such sense."

Brenna continues, "The antifreeze was right beside the boat launch. My dad said that people use antifreeze to winterize their boats and then flush the antifreeze out when they're ready to use the boat again in the spring."

Maggie adds, "Someone must have flushed it right there at the launch and not cleaned it up."

"And too many animals found it." Sunita's eyes tear up.

"So this was probably the work of an irresponsible boat owner," Maggie says. She closes the kittens' cage and writes on their chart.

Which means that now it's more important than ever that we get the word out about antifreeze. It's time to work on my PSA project with the Vet Volunteers.

Chapter Nine

· · · · · · · · · · · ·

It's way past lunchtime when we all invade Gran's fridge. I try to fix us something nutritious, but everyone seems too hungry to wait for real food. David and Maggie whip up boxed macaroni and cheese for everyone. The rest of us munch on carrots and apples while we wait for the microwave to serve up the orange cheesy mess.

"So, everybody, as I mentioned earlier today, I have a terrific plan for all of us," I say, tossing my apple core in the trash.

"Ahh, the mysterious PSAs?" Brenna asks.

"Exactly," I say. I fire up my laptop so I can show them the website I created.

"Well, spill it. Your first idea worked out great,"

David says between big bites of mac and cheese.

Before I can begin, David adds, "As a matter of fact, all of your ideas are great."

This remark seems to take everyone by surprise, even David himself, who immediately goes red in the face.

I need a moment to remember exactly what I was going to say. "We're going to film some public service announcements." I check to see if my computer is ready. Not yet. So I continue. "We'll do short commercials about animal health and safety. We can start with one about antifreeze. We'll post them on a couple of Internet video sites and on our own website. Then we can spread the word in the community so as many people as possible will see them. We can tell our friends and teachers at school, and put a link on the Dr. Mac's Place website. And Brenna, maybe your parents can help us get the word out at the wildlife rehab."

I look around Gran's kitchen to see how excited everyone is. Nobody really looks enthused.

David just looks confused. So does Josh. Sunita's eyes are wide and she is sitting up very straight. Jules's forehead is all scrunched up as she turns to look at Brenna. I can't tell what Brenna thinks, either. She's awfully quiet. I turn to look at my cousin. She doesn't look too excited, either.

"What do you mean, 'we're going to film them'?" asks Maggie. "With your Minicam?"

"Sure. It's a great little camera," I reply.

"Brian has one, too," David adds.

"Great, we can borrow his as well," I say. *And then I can see Brian, I think. Bonus!*

"Who are we filming doing this?" asks Jules.

"Yeah, who are the actors?" David asks.

"We are. That's what will make these really effective. Who cares about saving animals more than we do?"

Sunita nods slowly. Jules looks like she's starting to understand this, too.

"But—we're not actors," Jules says, sounding more than a little anxious.

"This isn't a movie," I say. "It's a short public service announcement. Acting in this sort of thing is easy. You just have to be yourselves."

"Don't you think we should hire some real actors, though?" Jules asks.

"No, I don't. Where would we get the money to pay them?" I look at my friends. Not one of them is excited like I thought they would be. "Don't you want to help teach people about antifreeze poisoning?"

Brenna speaks up. "Of course we do, Zoe. I think we're all just nervous about the acting part."

I try again to make them understand. "Listen, it's not like you have to become a character. It's not like being in a school play. We are Vet Volunteers, explaining something very important about animal care. It's nothing we haven't done lots of times. Just speak clearly and be yourselves." I look at David. "Or a calmer version of yourself."

"Ha!" he says, tossing a crumpled napkin at me.

I look from Vet Volunteer to Vet Volunteer. They all look nervous.

Then Brenna asks, "And what were you saying about the website?"

"Last night I set up a site for us," I say. "It's not much, but it's a start. We'll post the videos and create other content. We can write up other animal tips and even post pictures of animals that are available for adoption at the clinic, like those kittens were. Gran can help. She can make sure we've got it all right."

"Well, I'm in," Brenna says. "I think filming PSAs is a great idea. And I've always wanted to have a website for the Vet Volunteers."

"When are we going to do this? School starts back up tomorrow." Maggie doesn't look like she thinks this is such a good idea.

"Today," I reply. Everyone looks surprised. "Why not? I've written our first script. Once we do one, the rest will be easier. Then we can do a couple more next week."

"How many of these do you want us to do?" Sunita asks. She looks all kinds of worried again. I shouldn't be surprised, really. Sunita can be shy sometimes.

"We can start with one or two about the dangers of antifreeze. That way we have something to look at on our website. And then we'll do more as we come up with new topics." My computer is finally fully booted. I turn it so everyone can see the site.

"This looks great," Brenna says. "I like the pictures of Sherlock and the kittens. We might want to load a few more graphics up on it. I have a lot of wildlife images on my computer at home that we can use."

Josh leans in to look. "I like the puppy pictures on the home page."

Jules says, "We should take a picture of Cuddles for the site, too."

"And Rover," David chimes in.

"Yes, all great ideas," I say. "Now let's start the PSAs! The first one shoots in the backyard. Let's go."

We trample out to Gran's backyard. I give Maggie, Sunita, and Brenna one script to read over and Jules, Josh, and David the other. I should have made more copies. Oh well.

I scan the backyard for possible locations to film. Let's see. We could do it over by the tall evergreens, or maybe right beside the porch. And the lighting is really good down by the kennel runs. We'll try them all and pick the best ones to upload to the website. If we can at least get one done today, I can tell my mom to check it out. If all goes well, maybe I'll even get a response from her before I go to bed tonight.

"David, do you know how to use this?" I wave my camera.

"Yep. I used Brian's once when he didn't know. Took a video of him flexing his muscles in the mirror. Not much to look at."

"Did he find out?" Josh asks.

"Oh yeah. I got into some real trouble for that. But I know how to film." David turns back to me and reaches for my camera.

"Okay, well, let's start over by the trees. It'll make a nice background. Come on, everybody!" I lead the way to the farthest section of Gran's property.

To begin, I read the first line of the PSA in front of everyone as an example. I try to sound as natural as possible, while adding a little dramatic flair. I think it works, but the Vet Volunteers just kind of stare at me.

But that's ok. It's a simple PSA. Each of us has just one line of our own, and then we'll all read the last line in unison. Except for David, of course, since he's filming. Easy, right?

Except we can't seem to speak in unison.

And then David and Josh get a case of the giggles and Josh can't say his line at all, and David can't hold the camera straight while he laughs at Josh.

"I'm not so sure that this is working," Maggie says. "How many more times do we have to do it?"

"Should we have some kind of rehearsal?" Jules asks.

"I didn't think this would be too difficult," I say. "David, let me see what you've got so far."

David hands me my camera and I replay our attempts. The sound isn't great. We should shoot closer. The last take is too shaky to even consider, but even the first two tries seem jittery somehow. Then I see why.

"Sunita! You're wearing stripes," I say.

"Um, yeah," Sunita replies, looking down at her shirt.

"Stripes dance all over and shimmer on camera."

Sunita looks at me like she's never seen me before.

"You can't wear stripes on camera," I say. "Oh, and everybody, for the next time we shoot, wear solid colors, but not white or black. White draws too much attention, and black is hard to light. Jewel tones like ruby and emerald are the best. Stripes are out." I look over at Sunita. She shrugs.

"Also," I continue, "small and intricate designs are hard for the camera to read. Pastel shirts are fine, and the color blue is always good on TV. Don't wear jewelry that moves or makes noise. The microphone might pick it up. Dress simply. Oh, and no words or logos on your shirts. We don't want people reading your shirt instead of paying attention to our message!"

"Who knew when we got dressed today that we had to dress *for the camera*?" Maggie sighs. I make a mental note to help her pick out an outfit for next time. I'll probably have to lend her some of my clothes.

Gran calls to us from the back porch. "Do you kids want some lemonade?" She jiggles the glass in her hand. "I have a pitcher inside."

"We don't have time for a break!" I yell back. "We'll lose the light."

"Actually, Josh and I really have to get going," Jules says hesitantly.

"Me too," Brenna agrees. "We've had a long day."

"But what a great day!" Sunita says. "We found the antifreeze spill."

"But we don't have a single take that we can use yet. We need to go through it a few more times." I look at my friends. I can't believe that everyone is giving up so soon. The public needs to see these PSAs. And my mother needs to see them. She needs to see that what I'm doing is interesting, too.

"We'll get it right, Zoe. Let us know what time you want us next Saturday," Brenna says, tugging on her jacket.

"Next Saturday?"

"Spring break is over. We all have school tomorrow," Brenna explains. "Saturday is the soonest I can work on this again."

"Me too," Sunita says. "There's always extra homework when we get back from vacation."

Everyone is leaving, and we hardly got anywhere. Maggie walks with Brenna and pretends to dribble and shoot an imaginary basketball as she goes. Josh, Jules, David, and Sunita start heading back to the house, too. I feel miserable. I thought the PSAs were such a great idea, but everything is going wrong, and now we can't work on them for almost a whole week.

"David," Gran calls, "we should talk before you go." Her voice doesn't give much away, but she certainly didn't sound cheery. She turns and goes back into the house and—most likely—through to the clinic.

I look over at David. He is pale.

"Want me to come with you?" I ask. I am relieved when he nods. I don't know what Gran is about to tell him, but I think he could use a friend right now.

We walk back to the house in near silence. David usually tells a joke a minute, and he never just walks. David is a stone-kicker, a runner, a jump-around-like-a-baboon kind of guy. The fact that he's quietly walking tells me he is really nervous about Rover.

Maggie catches up with us in the house after saying good-bye to the others. She gently punches David in the shoulder. I know it's her way of telling him that she is there for him, too. The three of us enter the clinic together.

Gran is sitting on one of the high stools beside the cages in the recovery room and motions for David to do the same. Maggie and I stay standing. Gran's mouth is a straight line, but her eyes look soft. I am so nervous. What must David feel?

Finally, she begins. "I called your mom while you were all filming out back. I wanted to explain Rover's situation to her first and get some permissions."

Gran clears her throat. "David, Rover is a sick cat. He does not have antifreeze poisoning. But his condition is serious."

David tries to ask a question but does not get it out. Gran patiently waits, but then David just closes his mouth and looks out through his shaggy hair. She continues. "Rover has acute feline pancreatitis. I am treating him with plasma and I believe he will get better. But this is life-threatening, and we won't know how well he will respond to the treatment for a few more days."

David swallows. "How did he get it?" he manages to ask.

"It's hard to say," Gran answers. "Rover was a stray. There is so much that could have happened to him before you adopted him. Infection, insecticide exposure, a high-fat diet, trauma—a big fall, perhaps. It's likely we'll never know how he contracted this."

David nods.

Gran opens Rover's cage. Rover is hooked up to tubes and bags. "This is the plasma," she says, pointing to a large plastic IV bag. "I have him on a sedative because I need to give him the plasma without him pulling out the IV lines—as you all well know." She looks around at us. "And because feline pancreatitis is painful. Rover will heal faster if he is not in so much pain."

"Is that why he wasn't frisky anymore?" David asks.

"That's one reason. The other reason is that his organs were not working properly and he could not convert his food to energy." Gran rubs a finger along Rover's forehead and looks at David. "You know we'll take good care of him," she says. "Come over before school in the morning and help me with his lines. We'll know soon how he's going to do."

David nods again. "Thanks, Dr. Mac. See you in the morning." He waves good-bye to Maggie and me and crosses the recovery room floor. I've never seen him walk so slowly. The clinic feels much emptier as the door swings shut behind him.

"I'm going back in the house," I tell Maggie and Gran.

Gran wheels the full dirty linen cans toward the big washing machine. "Sure, Zoe, go on ahead. I won't be long."

"I'll help Gran get the laundry going," Maggie says. "Can you feed Sherlock for me?"

"No problem."

I walk down the hall and back into Gran's house. Oh. I suppose I should start thinking of it as my house, too. Sherlock gets to his feet when he sees me reach in the cupboard for his food. Scooping out the kibble makes me miss Sneakers even more. Sneakers thinks everything is a game, and he always gets so excited when it is time for his dinner. His tail wags like crazy and he jumps up and down and barks. Sherlock is much lazier. I watch as the basset hound wolfs his food down and then laps up his water, his tags jingling against the side of his bowl. For some reason, those jingling tags make me so sad. I wish I was listening to Sneakers's jingling tags with my mom in my home in California.

I decide to go to my room to see if Mom sent me an email.

She has, but it's another short one.

> Zoe, the weather continues its harassment of us. I have to imagine that this will extend our shooting time. Luckily, James keeps us all in high spirits. I hope your weather is better in Pennsylvania. You must be starting school tomorrow. Have a great time!
> Talk soon, Mom

Still no real conversation. No real news. Nothing even vaguely personal. She could have given that weather report as a tidbit to *People* magazine.

And hasn't it even occurred to her that starting at another school midyear might be something other than fun? She knows that I'm apprehensive about being back here. I don't know how long I sit there looking at the screen, or how long I've been crying. I only know that at some point Gran is beside me with tissues and hugs, and soon I'm closing my eyes in bed, feeling like I've cried out every drop of water in my body.

Chapter Ten

• • • • • • • • • • •

The next morning, Maggie walks with me to the school office but waits outside. My stomach feels a little wobbly and my forehead feels a little tight. I take a deep breath and walk inside.

In the office, the school secretary truly looks happy to see me.

"It's just wonderful to have you back with us, Zoe!" she says. "And I see you're as stylish as always."

"Thank you," I say. I'm wearing my new black-and-white polka-dot dress with my favorite pair of black suede cowboy boots. If Mom can't make me feel better, at least my shoes can.

The secretary flips open a folder and hands

me a large white-lined card and a class schedule. "Have your teachers sign the card as you go along, dear. Then just turn it in at the end of the day. Your mother and Dr. MacKenzie have you all re-registered, so I don't need anything else from you right now."

"Thank you," I say again and turn to leave.

"Zoe, you'll find we put you in Maggie's homeroom and a few other classes, too. Enjoy!" The secretary closes the folder and swivels her chair away as I leave the office.

"Cool!" Maggie says when she sees my schedule. "It'll be easier for you to help me with my homework if we're in the same classes."

That could be a good thing or a bad thing. I guess we're going to find out.

As we walk through the hallways, I hear lots of people call my name to say hello. There are more familiar faces than I expected. A couple of girls from my math class last year stop and excitedly ask me questions about Hollywood and where I got my boots. Maggie rolls her eyes, but I feel my shoulders relax a little. My stomach and head are already returning to normal. Maybe this won't be so bad. I'm good at school and I make friends pretty easily, and people seem happy to have me back. After all, I was worried about rejoining the

Vet Volunteers, and that seems to be working out fine.

After school, Maggie and I sit at Gran's kitchen table with Sherlock between us. We snack on apples and chunks of cheddar cheese. I look at a message that Gran has left for us.

> Girls, I'm assisting Dr. Gabe on a stable call. I should be back before 5. Get your homework done. And Zoe, your mom called. She got the time zone difference mixed up again. She said she'll try to reach you later. Love, Gran

This goes on for another two weeks. I leave phone messages for Mom, she leaves them for me. Mom sends me super short emails and I have a hard time replying to them. What can I say to her? School is school. She knows how the Vet Volunteers work. I could tell her about the antifreeze problem, but I want to wait until the PSAs are finished before I say anything. Nothing else is different, and I don't think anything will seem very interesting to her. Not when she's on a movie set with famous stars.

And our PSAs aren't any closer to being done. We haven't even been able to finish one about antifreeze, even though I have ideas for lots of others, like shelter adoption and spaying and neutering. Everyone is so busy, and when some of us do manage to get together to film one, something always goes wrong. Jules gets stage fright or David's jokes put everyone in stitches or the camera's battery is dead. I keep bugging David to see if we can use Brian's camera, but he shrugs me off. The videos aren't good enough to post, and they definitely aren't good enough for my mother to see.

Finally one night, Mom calls when I'm home. I've already gone to bed. Gran knocks on my door to see if I'm awake enough to take her call.

"Yes!" I say, throwing back the covers. Gran hands me the phone and leaves my room.

"Mom?" I'm so eager to hear her voice, but I'm also a little mad at her.

"Zoe! We're finally talking! This has been crazy, hasn't it?"

"It sure has. Don't they have clocks in Vancouver?"

Mom doesn't say anything for a moment. I only meant to tease a little. I think. But maybe I did want to hurt her a little as well.

"Mom?"

"Zoe, I'm doing my best here. Our shooting

schedule has been crazy. The weather is making it very hard to plan. We sit around for hours waiting to film only to have it called off for the day. And then we'll get a call to get to set with only a few minutes' notice. I have to stay in makeup all day just in case."

I hear her take a deep breath, and then she rushes on.

"Zoe, you know very well that some of these are remote location days. We talked about that before we left California. We don't have phone or Internet connections up there. It's very frustrating. James walks around with his iPhone out all day, hoping to get service, but it's just a lost cause."

"Mom?"

"Yes?"

"D-do you even miss me?" I stammer before my voice cracks with tears.

"Of course, baby, of course. I miss you terribly. How could I not? You're my only child. You're everything to me. But, sweetheart, you haven't exactly filled me in on things, either. You don't always reply to my emails."

"That's because I don't know what to say. Nothing about my life seems interesting enough to share when you're out making a movie," I choke out.

"Zoe, that's ridiculous. Everything about your life is interesting to me."

I guess I snort a little because she sighs and says, "Really, Zoe. You're my daughter. And I know you've heard it before, and you won't entirely believe it until you have a child of your own, but you are the most interesting, most important thing in my life. And you always will be."

"Even more interesting than this movie? Or your career? Or your new friend James?"

"Absolutely more interesting than all those things. Zoe, I love you fiercely," Mom says. And I believe her. Mostly.

"I love you too, Mom," I reply. I feel a little better.

"Now, baby, tell me what's going on in good old Ambler, Pennsylvania."

I fill Mom in on Maggie and Gran, on school and the Vet Volunteers. And then I bring up the PSAs. I wanted it to be a surprise, but at the rate we're going, who knows if we'll ever get them done. I may as well just tell her about them.

"I wanted to make these to help people understand. I wanted to help lots of animals," I explain.

I wonder if I should tell her the rest of it. I probably should. Mom has been honest with me; it's time I open up completely with her.

I fidget with the edge of my bedspread and say hesitantly, "I also wanted to have something important to show you so that you would want to be in touch with me more, to ask about how it was going. And so you would be proud of me. Kind of selfish, I know," I admit.

"Oh, Zoe." Mom sounds a little teary. "All of your reasons for those PSAs are good ones, and it sounds like a wonderful idea. But you don't have to try so hard to catch my attention. I'm sorry I haven't been good at showing you that I'm interested in your life, but I promise that I'm proud of you, no matter what. I'll talk to your grandmother and we'll set up a plan so we can keep in better touch, okay?"

Mom and I talk for another hour before she has to go back to work. It's after eleven here. I'm exhausted but also energized. I'm still uneasy about being in Ambler without Mom, but catching up with her has made me feel much better.

Chapter Eleven

. . . .

Two days later, when I arrive home from school, Gran takes my shoulders and ushers me into my room. On my desk is my computer with a small camera clipped to the top. And on the screen is my mother!

We start to talk but have a little trouble. The screen freezes up when Mom begins to talk, and it takes a couple of tries before our connection works properly. But now it's running smoothly. Mom looks great. She's in full movie makeup. But I'm sure the sweater she is wearing is part of her costume. She'd never wear anything so dreary in real life.

"Nice outfit, Mom," I tease.

"Ha! Special just for you," she says. She straightens her sweater and fluffs her hair.

I stand and twirl and show her my outfit. Then I strike a red-carpet pose like she taught me.

"What do you think?" I ask.

"You look perfect to me," she replies. "Absolutely perfect."

We smile at each other and wave. It's great to be able to see her face and not just her emails.

"Now, Zoe, I have a little surprise for you. I've set up some help for you and your friends."

Mom is grinning. What is she talking about?

She goes on. "One of the local news stations in Philadelphia is going to film the PSAs for you! They'll even run some on the station before and after the morning and evening news."

"You're kidding! That's great! Everyone is going to be so excited." I'm actually not sure about that, but I know I can talk them into doing it anyway. I'll have to. How fun!

"Oh, and Zoe," Mom continues, "my friend James is flying down to help. He isn't in the next few scenes that are shooting this week. I'm sure you'll all make him feel welcome."

I can see her quizzical look clearly. She wants me to be extra nice to James. Hmmm. Sounds like he might be turning into more than a friend. I don't know how I feel about that.

The next week, at the news station, we are a jittery cluster of Vet Volunteers. Gran looks nervous, and she isn't even acting. The evening news anchorwoman has been enlisted to help us.

"Hi, kids, I'm Ginny," she introduces herself, smiling. "It's great to see you. We'll do a quick rehearsal, and then get you into makeup."

David and Josh look horrified.

"It's just news makeup," she reassures the boys. "No eye shadow or anything. All the men wear it when they're on camera. It's mostly to keep the cameras from picking up too much shine from your skin. We'll be sure to help you take it off before you leave." The boys nod reluctantly, but they don't look happy.

I, on the other hand, am excited about the makeup. Mom's makeup artists used to give me makeovers if I was on set. Even though Mom usually told them to "tone it down a bit," it always looked good and it was nice to feel pampered.

I lean over to Jules. "Just wait until you see how good a makeup artist can make you look!"

She doesn't reply, and she looks a little sick.

"It's going to be okay," I say encouragingly. "Just look at the camera and imagine that you're talking to a friend about something you care about very much."

"Exactly!" Ginny has overheard me. "Everyone? Everyone? Gather 'round. Let's all think about what, um, what is your name, sweetie?"

"Zoe."

"Let's all think about what Zoe said," Ginny continues. "You're going to look at the camera and pretend that the camera is a friend. You'll talk to the camera just like you're talking to a friend. I've read your PSA spots and they are perfect."

She turns to me and says, "I think the professional actor is already here. He stopped in last night from the airport and all the ladies were quite flustered."

Interesting. I imagined he'd be good-looking. I'm glad I'll be able to check him out, especially now that I suspect he's more than just my mom's friend.

Ginny leads us into the studio. The evening news set is pushed up against one wall. It looks so much smaller here than it does on TV. Two stools are set up in front of a deep-blue background.

"Let's rehearse once with just the kids," Ginny says to the cameraman. We rehearse, and it goes much better than it did in Gran's backyard, even though most of my friends seem nervous. Maybe it's because this setting is so professional. Or maybe it's because the anchorwoman is better at directing than I am. No, I think the real reason is that now all we have to do is recite one line in unison. Now that James is involved, he'll be reading the rest of the lines by himself. I guess Jules was right after all—this is much easier with a professional actor involved.

Then Ginny looks at the clock on the wall and waves us all to follow her.

"It's time to get into makeup. We need to be quick," she says. "Come with me."

They decide to do the boys' makeup first. Josh sits through it just fine. David is in the second chair, squirming as though the makeup stings him. He can be so ridiculous. The girls go next, one after another. Maggie usually hates makeup, but I see her sneaking a small smile at herself in the mirror when she's done. Finally, it's my turn, and I like the results! My skin is glowing and my cheeks are pink. I bet I'll look good on camera.

It's time to go into the studio, and I can't believe it, but I actually feel butterflies in my stomach. This is really happening. David and Josh push each other around as we walk in the hall. Sunita's eyes are extra huge, and it's not from the makeup. I feel bad that she looks so scared. Even Brenna is pretty quiet. Ugh. This is supposed to be fun for everyone, not torture.

I look around as we enter the studio. There are so many extra adults in the room. They must be employees because they have ID badges on cords around their necks. They look anxious, too. But I don't see the famous James anywhere. Anchorwoman Ginny lines us up behind the two stools. I wonder why there are two. James needs just the one, I would think.

There is some kind of commotion behind us, but I can't immediately see what's going on. The camera blocks my vision.

"Who is that?" I hear.

One of the adults gasps, "It's him."

I turn around to see a tan guy with a tousled haircut, perfectly rumpled jeans, and a slightly too-small black T-shirt that hugs his biceps. Yep, he's Hollywood all right. This must be James. I think I recognize him, actually. He's been in a few movies. No wonder the studio is filled with employees. They all want to meet the famous actor.

And then—no, I can't believe it. I see someone even more famous! Famous to me, anyway. My mother!

"Zoe! Surprise!" She races toward me and whips me into a hug.

I look up at her. It's real. She's here. She looks

gorgeous in a deep-purple blouse and fitted black skirt, with her hair and makeup all done up. My mom.

"Are you surprised?" She hugs me again. "Did anyone breathe a word about my coming?"

"Gran didn't say a thing." I look over to where my grandmother is standing with the TV station people. Gran gives me a thumbs-up. Mom squeezes my arm.

Anchorwoman Ginny rushes up. "Are we ready to start?"

Mom nods. "James, shall we?"

He stops shaking hands with the station employees and flashes her a smile. Then he jogs over.

"You must be Zoe," he says exuberantly. "I'm so pumped to meet you. Your mom has told me so much about you."

She has?

I hardly have time to process what's happening when the cameraman says, "Okay, kids, you know your lines. We're going to get a fix on you for the camera and then we'll give you the go-ahead to start. And make sure you speak a little slower than you normally do. Most people tend to talk too fast because they're nervous."

Well, now I *am* nervous! Extremely nervous.

I never thought we'd be doing this in front of so many people. Including my mom. I glance at Maggie. She looks worse than I feel.

Then we begin.

JAMES: *"Tens of thousands of pets are killed every year because of antifreeze poisoning. Antifreeze poisons over two thousand children each year."*

MOM: *"It takes just one or two tablespoons of antifreeze to kill a dog and as little as one teaspoon to kill a cat. As little as one or two tablespoons of antifreeze can be lethal to toddlers and small children, and even a taste can result in hospitalization. Check your garage floors for antifreeze leaks."*

JAMES: *"If you own a boat, be careful not to drip or flush antifreeze into our water or onto our shores."*

MOM: *"Many states have enacted legislation requiring the addition of a bittering agent to antifreeze. This makes antifreeze taste so terrible that it drastically reduces the likelihood that a child or animal would be poisoned by it."*

JAMES: *"Urge your lawmakers to fight for this legislation. Call or write them today!"*

VET VOLUNTEERS: *"Antifreeze is sweet, attractive, and deadly. But antifreeze poisoning is preventable. Do your part."*

We have to go through it twice to get it right. But then Ginny yells, "Cut!" and we're done!

The Vet Volunteers cheer. James gives Mom

a hug. Longer than just a friend's hug, I'd say. Maggie catches my eye. She saw that hug, too. I think Maggie and I have another popcorn-fueled cousin catch-up night in store.

After the taping, Mom and James take all of the Vet Volunteers (and Gran, of course) out for a great meal at the nicest restaurant in town. James tells us all about how the production team at the news station will edit the PSA. Once they're done, we'll all get a copy and they'll let us know when it will air on TV. I still can't believe it—the Vet Volunteers, on television! Then, after a night of gossiping with Maggie, I get to make brunch with Mom, just the two of us. Whole-wheat French toast with organic mixed berries—yum! Unfortunately right after that, Mom has to head back to Vancouver, and I've barely had a full twenty-four hours with her. I'm a little sad about it, but she and Gran and I spent some quality time with the calendar, writing things down and making plans. I'm going to visit Mom in Vancouver and we're even going to have a getaway weekend in New York City. So that's pretty good for now.

The next day, David comes to the clinic to take Rover home. The formerly frisky cat has made a full recovery. Maggie and I are handling Rover in the recovery room while Gran goes over the post-

clinic care instruction sheet with David. Rover
squirms and jumps out of Maggie's lap, making
a beeline for David. He drops the sheet, and as
it flutters to the floor, Rover jumps and catches
it in his mouth. The cat takes off, racing around
the room with the paper dangling beneath his
whiskers. It's so good to see him back to normal.

"Rover, sit," David calls. Rover sits. "Rover,
come." Rover trots right over to David, and David
takes the paper from him. "Good boy, Rover, good
boy," David says with a big grin as he scratches
his cat under the chin. I think David is back to
normal, too.

"That is one strange cat you've got there," I say
to David.

"One of a kind," David agrees, and lifts Rover
into the cat carrier.

"One of a kind. Just like you, Zoe," Maggie
says, eyeing my outfit. What? My floral dress and
moccasins are totally on trend.

David takes off with Rover, and Maggie and I
head back to the house. It's time for lunch.

"So, Maggie," I say sweetly, "I've made a
vegetarian quinoa bowl with cucumber, tofu, and
avocado. It has a sesame-ginger dressing, and I've
topped it with nori and sunflower sprouts."

"That almost sounds good enough to try without

holding my nose," Maggie says, poking my arm playfully. "Come on Gran, Zoe has whipped us up another treat."

I grab a box of Pop-Tarts from the cupboard and toss them to Maggie.

"Just in case you don't like it. We do have fallback food," I say.

Maggie laughs and tosses the box up in the air and catches it again.

"I'm kind of getting used to your weird food, Zoe. I think we can stash these for now."

Gran is pulling a pitcher out of the refrigerator. "Homemade iced pomegranate white tea," she says, proudly holding it up for me to see. "Your mom told me it was your favorite. It wasn't much harder to make than that instant lemonade I usually mix up."

I beam at my grandmother. I love that my mom was thinking of me, and I love that Gran made the tea. The three of us get the table ready for lunch. Maggie pulls out the plates, I prepare the quinoa, and Gran pours our healthy drinks. And for the first time in a long while, I feel we aren't just acting like a family. We really are one.

LAURIE HALSE ANDERSON

In addition to the Vet Volunteers series, Laurie Halse Anderson is the author of the multiple award-winning, *New York Times* bestselling novel *Speak*, as well as *Catalyst* (an ALA Top Ten Best Book for Young Adults), *Prom*, *Twisted*, and *Wintergirls* (all *New York Times* bestsellers), and is the recipient of the Margaret A. Edwards Award for her contributions to young adult literature. Additionally, Laurie's historical novels about early America—*Fever 1793*, *Chains*, and *Forge*—are taught in schools around the country. You can visit Laurie online at www.madwomanintheforest.com.